CW00731885

Nancy and the Count

Nancy and the Count

Vampires' Gold

Frank Merryfellow

Frogmort Press

Frogmort Press
first printing 2023

print ISBN -
9786165988568
e-book ISBN -
9786165988407

BISAC Subject Headings -
FIC031070 FICTION / Thrillers / Supernatural
FIC009050 FICTION / Fantasy / Paranormal
FIC042080 FICTION / Christian / Fantasy

Cover art – Design Zaw Oo

Frank Merryfellow lives in Chiang Mai, northern Thailand. This is his first novel.

Dear reader,

At heart, this is a story of good and evil.

There are scenes of violence and depravity. But I believe that our protagonist, dear Nancy, will see us through.

The action appears to take place in a reality adjacent to our own – but I only know what Nancy tells me.

- Merryfellow

Prologue - southeast Burma, August 1945

It is three weeks before the end of World War Two. The Japanese Imperial Army is retreating from Burma.

In the past few months, small detachments of English officers have parachuted in behind enemy lines with radios and rifles. In the hills, they are mobilising bands of ethnic Karen fighters to ambush the retreating Japanese army.

Having abandoned Rangoon, the Japanese withdraw across the Sittaung River and down the valley, blowing the bridge behind them. The retreat is ragged and desperate, as they pick up stragglers from the hills.

Meanwhile, militias from the ethnic Burman majority have attacked Karen villages across the country, calling them lackeys of the colonial regime. There have been massacres.

Realising that they will never have a place in a country dominated by the Burmans, well-armed and trained Karen soldiers from the British regular and irregular forces have started organising for independence of their homeland after the war. First though, they have to help the allies defeat Japan.

...

Papun town - gateway to the Karen hills. The last Japanese units are withdrawing, racing to join retreating columns to the southwest before the British and Empire Forces cut them off. The once busy market is almost deserted.

On a hillside above the little town, a sparkling golden chedi on a white marble platform. Not far from the pagoda, close to where the bamboo-fringed jungle begins, a large, roofless mansion – Harlan House, recently and accidentally bombed by the RAF.

It is late afternoon, warm and damp; frogs croak.

Sir Roger Silk, secret agent and vampire, squats on a stool, outside a tent pitched on what was once the croquet lawn. He is slim and tall, pale and dark-haired, possibly in his 30s. In each hand, a small object, one white one green. He notices Lt. Yakamoto watching him. Beyond, a small group of soldiers and locals prepare rice and yams for dinner.

Silk pockets the small objects. He had wanted to feel the smooth stones in his hand, cool as his blood. Normally, he would not be so indiscreet. However, these men will not live to see the dawn.

Last night he glimpsed it - just before sunrise. A glint of gold beneath the flag-stones. Bats wheeling overhead. Not his bats – but that is of little concern, for now.

A brass bell chimes nearby – returning the vampire to the present.

"I'm off for a stroll before dinner. Won't be long." Silk rises softly.

"A stroll - really? Don't let the busted catch you."

He won't. Silk feels his strength returning as evening approaches.

He can walk in the daylight, albeit uncomfortably under a wide-brimmed hat, well-covered like a proper English colonial. But in the sun his powers are much diminished, and direct sunlight will burn and eventually kill him.

Silk will wait for dark, then gather his band of Familiars, and two soldiers who are bound to him in blood.

He has orders from Tokyo, impeccably forged. But Yakamoto is suspicious - has noticed that Silk never eats – at least, not food. And he sleeps under guard for much of the day.

This Yakamoto seems a decent type. Disappointing.

Silk and his party will slip away tonight, while the lieutenant is sleeping.

...

By midnight, the gold is disinterred - slung onto a dozen donkeys. The flag-stones are artfully re-laid.

A few hours earlier, Lt. Yakamoto had come upon them, sword drawn. But he didn't stand a chance. A broken neck, poor Yakamoto.

Silk knows that the two Japanese soldiers are horrified, but they are under his power and can do nothing.

They are up into the hills now, to find a likely cave - "To which we will return when better armed." Possibly they believe him.

Beautiful up here by moonlight – wooded hills and bamboo groves above Papun. On to the limestone outcrops in the deeper forest - trail-end of the Himalayas; full of grottos, springs and caves.

He works his Familiars and slaves hard to re-inter the gold and rubies before dawn.

Now Silk will kill them all. He's been working up an appetite.

Part One – London

Chapter 1

Bats wheel round a clump of beech trees, beneath streetlights. A storm recedes to the north. Across the road in her 8th floor flat, Nancy wakes.

The dream evaporates, leaving the same image of a small but precious object - green, alluring - which has disturbed her for years. But this time there is something else - a fragment, glowing sickening red.

Nancy senses it is just before dawn, and her alarm clock will soon go off.

When it does, she shifts out of bed to the sounds of Radio One. The familiar pain in her head, and down her right leg.

It's cold up here. And lonely. As almost every morning, Nancy wishes she had a pet cat. Not allowed.

Last night's cold rice and curry for breakfast. Into the shower, then prayer.

Nancy prayed for her people and her family, for protection and justice - and above all in gratitude for Grace.

She traced the scar from her crown to her brow, a bit below the hair-line. Pain nagging in the background. She touched the scars on her legs and lower back, where a dozen lumps of shrapnel had been so painfully removed. Half a decade after she last went under the knife, Nancy could still feel tiny phantom balls of burning iron.

She put a heavy-duty jacket on over jeans and hoodie, tucked her medium-length almost black hair into a bike helmet. As usual, the lift wasn't working, so Nancy walked down to street level.

South into London, through Finsbury Park and past the Arsenal Stadium she sped. This bicycle was the most expensive thing Nancy owned. Her comrades, dead and dispersed, would understand the need to keep fit, and above all to stay sane - so she didn't feel too guilty about buying it.

Eyes on the road though. She liked watching people on the pavements, especially families. But careful not to be distracted.

Twenty-four minutes after leaving home (almost her record), Nancy pulled into the staff car park, round back of the university main entrance - just in time to be nearly knocked off her bike by Professor Grim in his Tesla. He didn't bother saying sorry. She felt almost invisible - which in some ways was quite comforting.

...

Yesterday at church, Auntie May had teased that she needed a boyfriend. Nancy thought she did not.

"I'm quite capable of coping without a man. Thank you."

Auntie May was right though: she was lonely. But the prospect of romance with someone from church, or work, seemed unlikely. So last night she had set up a dating app profile, and submitted it before she could reconsider – but she would delete the app when she got home tonight. Just a bit of harmless fun; this was not the way to meet a nice young man.

Nancy slipped on her overalls, before locking the bike. Through the swing doors to pick up her kit.

Usually she started early evenings, and worked until midnight. Today she had a 'bonus shift', with just two hours break between this extra period and her usual round of night-time cleaning and sweeping. The additional income was welcome, and she liked seeing people in the usually empty offices and seminar rooms.

First stop: reception area and the secretaries' offices. Nancy knew that it was silly to be proud of working at - or rather, for - Ladbroke College. After all, she was a cleaner, on contract to an outside company. She liked the atmosphere though, and the people here mostly treated her kindly. Much nicer than the empty offices she had cleaned for years, before the agency moved her here. And nicer also than Frogmort Manor (especially at the end), where Auntie May had found a job for her a few years back.

There were curiosities aplenty at the Department of History and Archaeology. Her friend Lilly over at the medical school said she was terrified of the skeletons and anatomical models encountered on her cleaning rounds. Nancy however, enjoyed being around the ancient pots and other bits and pieces, stacked on shelves and benches. She had developed an interest in some of these old artefacts, even looking up a few objects on Wikipedia. Last week, she had felt well-enough informed to ask Prof Pratt - who seemed approachable - about the small statuette on his desk. She knew she wasn't supposed to talk to the academics, but sensed he wouldn't mind.

"The Egyptian goddess Isis – adopted by the Romans. Replica of the Duclan find, dug up from the mud of the Thames riverbank in – er – 1995?

The original is in the British Museum. Just across Rutland Square."

He gestured out the window, beyond which the museum stood almost visible through months of London grime. She had never visited.

"Can I ask why you enquire?"

Something about the cool white stone was comforting. Nancy was confident the professor had not noticed her having handled it a couple of times. No harm done.

"I don't know Professor - just it's very beautiful, and I was curious.

Sorry to take up your time Sir."

"That's quite all right - Nancy, did you say?

"I'm always happy to chat with people who are interested.

Say hello any time you're passing."

Nancy smiled, bowed her head and slipped away. She looked back to see Pratt tapping away at his computer.

Nancy picked empty crisp packets, broken ballpens and screwed-up paper from office trash cans. Later that morning she told the Professor she had looked up Isis on the internet and ordered a book on the subject.

"During my break, of course."

"That's excellent Nancy.

Did you know that Sally – sorry, as of last month, Dr Weston - here" - indicating a passing colleague - "is quite an expert on the goddess.

Sally, meet Nancy - our scholarly janitor."

Nancy nodded towards the young woman in pink jeans and beige blouse, a lick of blonde hair curling over her brow - "Good morning."

"Good morning Nancy. Very nice to meet you.

The goddess is quite beautiful, isn't she. Did you know that, after her husband was murdered and dis-membered, she reconstructed his body?"

Nancy didn't know what to do with that. "Oh - how interesting."

Other than that, she was mostly on her own throughout the day.

After work, a bit of shopping, before heading back to Tattenham. She shouldn't have bought such a large jug of cooking oil. It nearly tipped out of her bicycle basket.

After getting home and stowing her goods, Nancy washed her face and hands before turning to her phone. She paused at the small hall-way mirror. She supposed she was still pretty, in an ordinary way – and skinny. The scar showed a bit less than in the past. It was grey-ish now, rather than the searing pink of earlier years. Auntie May said it made her look "distinguished" - a word Nancy had looked up, which didn't seem particularly suited to a young lady.

She bunched her hair into a bun, fastened with a bunny-clasp. Her temple throbbed again. She paused before picking up her phone. Nancy was surprised to see several responses to her profile. Out of politeness, she scrolled through each of them before deleting.

The last one was undeniably intriguing: Roger Silk (if that was his real name) - dark, pale and handsome. How had he managed to skip so many categories? His profile didn't even include an age. There was not much to go on, beyond interests in sacred history and Burmese politics.

...

Two days later, she bumped into Professor Pratt again - literally. Or rather, he into her.

"I'm so sorry, Nancy. Very clumsy of me.

Please, let me get you another one of those."

He indicated her toppled sandwich, squashed on the lecture hall floor.

"And while I do so, let me introduce an old friend.

Our guest speaker tonight - Dr Jakob Van Helsing."

A trim middle-aged man was approaching - a crest of white hair, in a light grey three-piece suit and blue necktie. A silver medallion on a watch-chain, half concealed beneath his jacket. When he smiled at Nancy, a flash of steel in those pale blue eyes.

"Very pleased to meet you, Miss - ?"

"I'm Nancy. Pleased to meet you sir.

I'm very much looking forward to your talk this evening."

"Why thank you Nancy.

I'm really just a collector of folk tales. Something of a hobby, but it keeps me out of trouble - and makes a change from the day job."

Nancy knew he was a journalist, or something like that - apparently quite well known.

"Anyway - I hope you will enjoy the lecture."

"Oh yes.

'Colonial Spooks - Ghost Stories from Imperial Burma and Indonesia'. I've ordered the book already."

"That's very good of you.

You will have to track me down - or I you. You must let me sign your copy at least. You will have to let me know what you think of it.

There are strange things out there, Nancy."

Prof. Platt returned with fresh sandwiches.

"Ah - Peter, don't mind if I do.

Now - you were going to tell me how you're getting on at the castle. Have you come up with anything interesting?"

...

Three nights later, Nancy prepared for her date. She wasn't sure why she had agreed. But then again - why not? She was a grown woman, and a good Christian.

Silk had suggested they meet at La Parla, a little Italian restaurant off Rutland Square - convenient for her after work (although presumably he didn't know where she worked?). She checked the place out before saying yes. It seemed harmless enough.

As his profile suggested, Silk was young-ish, posh and English. He cut a handsome if out-of-date figure, in a pale linen suit. He was polite and attentive, but not overly so. Cool and confident. She liked that – sort of.

He both repelled and attracted. Nancy didn't know if this was normal for an Englishman, but she found it quite disturbing. And also compelling. Probably she was overthinking it. After all, she hadn't been on a date for years.

Nancy relaxed, and allowed herself a glass of wine over dinner (ravioli in tomato sauce); Silk drank what he said was whiskey. He was apologetic. Just this afternoon, he had been notified of a slot open tomorrow for minor surgery. He had been on the waiting list for so long, and had to take this opportunity. It wasn't an emergency, but serious enough to mean he couldn't eat with her tonight. But he insisted that Nancy should dine.

"I'm sure you understand. And of course, we don't have each other's numbers - which is as it should be - but that meant I couldn't call and let you know."

Ridiculous, but what can she say.

Silk was very handsome. And the restaurant was nice – proper linen on the tables and heavy cutlery. Not like the staff canteen at the university. The waiter seemed to know him. At first Nancy thought that was just pretending, maybe to get a tip or something - but she could tell there was some connection between them. Both so pale and dark - slightly shimmering somehow, especially Silk.

Nancy couldn't recall much of what they talked about. Silk was an amateur historian, a collector - "To be honest, a dilettante" (whatever that meant).

He was very curious about the department - particularly regarding a castle to the north of London. Presumably the one which Dr Van Helsing had mentioned. According to Silk, some kind of survey was being led by one Peter Pratt.

"I think that's his name, anyway. I read about it somewhere. And you mentioned that you work at the university."

Silk seemed disappointed that, although she had met the Professor, Nancy knew little about his work. He expressed great interest in her background in Burma - "or Myanmar, if you prefer". (She didn't.)

Not many of the English she met had much knowledge of her

country. But that was hardly a good reason to accompany the stranger back to his apartment.

She had never done anything like this before. Had he spiked her drink? She supposed it was possible. But the shimmering had started as soon as she met him.

Nancy could more or less re-construct the conversation, but still couldn't fathom why she had gone with him. She was indeed interested in photographs of Burma in the old days - the colonial period. Apparently, Silk had a collection of prints and lithographs. He had more recent photos also - from before 2021, when the country had seemed to be recovering from decades of military mis-rule. Before the army plunged it back again into violence and chaos. Those green dogs.

Nancy found it hard to concentrate. He was talking, or was she talking - she couldn't follow the words. The shimmering was coming in waves; her vision began to break up – a dark fractal vortex.

Nancy swooned, finding herself in his arms. What a cool embrace. He must have moved so quickly.

Silk grinned - a flash of fang. Not knowing why, Nancy threw back her head, exposing her throat.

The room grew darker, crazy angles collapsing through her field of vision. The wood-panelled walls bent to weird dimensions.

She caught the glint of his eye – a glittering fang.

This is not what she wants – not at all.

She has so little strength – just enough to push him away, a few inches.

"No - not this, not this."

He forced her back down onto the divan.

Silk was sickening, and incredibly strong – waves of shimmering nausea.

He loomed above her, ready to swoop.

Nancy remembered the jungle – fumbling and groping - a smelly new recruit trying his luck. She punched upwards into Silk's lower jaw.

Her fist connected - Silk drew back in surprise. A chance to slide out from underneath.

Nancy staggered towards a large marble fireplace, bruising her shoulder as she crashed into the mantle. She turned back towards the monster on the couch. His golden eyes suffused with a compulsive power.

Silk jumped up, licked his suddenly scarlet lips and moved so swiftly towards her. The glimmering vortex. She began to swoon again - but resisted the urge, the surge of collapsing black fractals.

Nancy shot out her left arm to steady herself. The vampire was drawing upwards again to strike. He had grown impossibly taller. The lights flickered - supercharged static in the air.

Stumbling, she grabbed an iron poker from its stand by the cold fireplace - stepped back, desperately extending it in front of her.

Silk pounced, with fangs drawn - and she drove the fire-poker deep into the vampire's chest.

He shot upwards. An awful screeching, then gurgling – suspended in mid-air, writhing beneath the high ceiling. A wrenching jolt and screech of agony and despair.

Blood spurted out of him - over her, over the walls and much of the furniture.

An almighty crash, as the fiend slammed down onto the floor awash with blood.

Nancy stepped smartly back, avoiding much of the gore – but she almost slipped in the stinking stuff.

She regained her balance. The vampire was slumped on the floor in a crimson-black pool - the poker driven through his heart.

Nancy's head was pounding. She wanted to vomit, but didn't.

...

Seduced by a vampire. But not successfully, or fatally.

Blood everywhere.

Nancy was lightheaded, but not so swoony.

She prayed for a long time, asking for guidance. She gave thanks for the protection she had received, and blessed the name of Jesus.

She knew this – thing - was a vampire, without knowing quite how she knew. Maybe from those movies and TV shows she had watched in her first years in England, trying to pick up idioms and a feel for the culture (not realising at first that Buffy was American). Nancy knew that vampires drink blood, and are unholy ("undead" - that was the word). But that was about all she could remember. Quite rightly, they were afraid of the cross.

Standing up again, she surveyed the bloodstains and clots - large pools of the stuff spreading from the corpse. Would a neighbour call the police? He had made so much noise!

How could there be so much blood?

It was her fault he was dead. But he had attacked her. And anyway, he was a vampire.

Good luck explaining that to the police!

This could go very badly. She didn't feel like one, but perhaps she was a murderer - if it was possible to murder the undead.

Nancy told herself to examine the corpse. Expensive tailoring, as far as she could tell - soaked in blood from the waist up. She prodded him (it?) with her foot, noticing as he rolled over that the fangs had receded. A young-ish dead white man. Not the first corpse she had seen, nor the most disfigured - but the first dead westerner. And certainly her first vampire.

Nancy's temple began to throb. For once, she was grateful for the pain.

She had been lucky - or rather, blessed. Time to get out of here. There was no way she could clean up all this mess, and what on earth would she do with the body anyway?

Nancy was becoming fearful as much of legal consequences as the mortal kind. She went to the cavernous marble bathroom, stripped and showered. No soap or towels to be seen. Afterwards, she had no alternative but to put her bloodied clothes back on.

Back in the room where the vampire lay dead, Nancy saw two half-empty wine glasses. She didn't remember drinking after they got back to the apartment. Nancy did remember that the immigration and naturalisation authorities had her fingerprints on file. She poured red wine onto the floor, then put the fine-cut glasses into her shoulder bag, retrieved from the hallway. She would dispose of these later.

Nancy found a dish-cloth in the kitchen. (The fridge was on, but empty.) She wiped carefully around places where she might have left traces. She had learnt something from those detective shows.

Nancy knew she should get out soon, but first a quick look round the apartment. Larger, and more high-class than any she had been in before. Lots of marble and polished floors, but not much else. Minimal furniture. Two empty bedrooms and three rooms with locked doors.

She went back to stand over his body. This was the only properly furnished room.

Nancy offered a prayer for Silk's soul. Then looked around some more.

No sign of a computer or electronic devices. Mostly history and art books on the shelves.

On a huge oak table at the back of the room, and a small stack of papers. Advertising brochures for soil enrichment companies. A few leaflets about nuclear fallout shelters. Two volumes of an academic journal on Southeast Asian history - the latter resting on a large white envelope.

The envelope was clearly unsealed.

Inside, a dozen A4-sized glossy photographs. Views of the security gates and the back of the university.

Why on earth would he have photos of Ladbroke College?

Half-a-dozen photos of a castle. Then two clear images of her, Nancy, in overalls at work – telephoto lens. A couple of Prof. Pratt and one of Sally Weston. And three or four photos of broken down old places she didn't recognise.

Beneath a crystal paperweight, a small hardback notebook. She hesitated, then slipped this out.

The notebook was less than half-filled with spidery handwriting, in black and sometimes blue ink. Most of it seemed to be in a foreign language. A European script.

She picked out some phrases in English –

White Tiger, Green Dragon.
Beneath the Burmese Bell.
Before the C- awakes.

Undated, but the faded ink looks old.

Her heart quickened when she saw the 'apple core' Burmese script, beautifully transcribed. Some street and pagoda names from Yangon (or Rangoon, as it was then) - what looked like notes on a railway timetable; lists of names, male and female; something about a murder.

That phrase again –

Beneath the Burmese Bell.

And then –

Papun!

Heart of the revolution, home of the brave Karen rebels.

Too much to take this in just now. She had better leave before the police arrive.

Nancy stuffed the notebook into her pocket, then checked herself for remaining bloodstains. No mirrors in this place! She had better get going.

Thank goodness her long raincoat was hanging by the doorway still. As she reached for the coat, Nancy's eye was drawn to a small ebony stand next to the big black door, in the middle of which was an exquisitely carved, two-inch tall white marble tiger. Nancy slipped it into her coat pocket, straightened her hair.

Why did I do that?

She stepped out into the night - expecting any moment to hear sirens.

Nearby there was a night-bus route she knew. Thank goodness. Thank God.

...

Although it was close to midnight, Nancy got off a few stops from her flat, in front of Bethnay Baptist Church. The large blue wooden doors were immediately comforting.

Nancy had thought to pray on the church steps, then wait for the next night bus in 20 minutes. She was sure she would be safe at church.

She hadn't expected the doors to be open - but one was ajar, with dim lights on inside.

She was not frightened - but Nancy thought it might be improper to enter this holy place smeared with vampire's blood. She prayed for guidance, trusting that God would understand.

Then she peered inside.

There was someone at the far end of the building - semi-crouched in the shadows, facing away from her. He straightened, and turned towards her - not too tall, but obviously strong. He blinked stepping into the brighter light, and slowly smiled.

Saw Wah! The best possible person to meet at this time.

Nancy cleared her throat a bit self-consciously, and proceeded into the church.

Saw Wah had been working with a saw and chisels on the front pews. He helped out when he could at church and in the community, after his day job.

In Karen - "Good evening, Thramu Nancy.

Are you okay? You don't look very well."

His flat, open face, quite handsome.

...

Seven hours after Nancy annihilated the vampire Silk, two dozen miles to the northeast, a slab of ancient brickwork came loose and fell from the battlements of Broglin Castle, near Waltham Abbey on the edge of Epping Forest. It crashed through the rusty guttering, smashing into the ground below. Soon afterwards, a second larger chunk of stone broke away, skidding down the steep zinc roofing. It landed directly on Sheila Brighton, killing her instantly on the way to work.

Sheila was deputy day-manager at the Broglin Castle Hotel, which occupied the more modern wing, to which the old castle was attached. Her head and upper body were pulverised. Blood over the old walls, the new asphalt, and along a gravel path connecting the rear of the hotel to a large car park, and beyond that the lake. Considering the destruction caused, the incident was largely silent - the impact of falling stanchion mostly muffled in compressing Sheila.

The sun came up over gobbets of flesh and bone, pools of blood soaking into the pebbles and ornamental flowerbeds. One of the staff found the body after the night shift ended.

After discreet discussions with the police, hotel management agreed that the day's busy programme - a corporate lunch, and in the afternoon a society wedding - need not be overly disrupted by this terrible accident. A cordon was set around the incident site and pathways leading round the old castle were blocked off. For the next few days at least, guests would have to walk around the lawn to reach their cars.

...

Prof Pratt was alerted while travelling to work on the bus. He cancelled the departmental meeting, and set off for Broglin by Uber, arriving some hours before the rest of his team, who had been due to start work after lunch. It was quickly determined that the mortar and cement used in the oldest parts of the castle roof had given out in the recent hot weather. Last night's storm had dislodged a loose knob of ancient stone and cement.

Last year he had pointed out that rising temperatures were affecting the integrity of the structure, particularly the upper parts of the castle, which had not been properly inspected or secured in decades. It seemed the drying process had accelerated in the hot months since he was last up on the roof. Not surprising that Prof. Pratt's findings had failed to result in action. Across the country, private citizens and public bodies were scrambling to stave off the impacts now or later of rising tides and temperatures.

Pratt tried to resist two selfish thoughts: this proved he was right about the need for a proper survey of the castle - but also, this would lead to further delays. His team were already behind schedule in documenting, and where possible beginning light conservation work on the upper interior. Having stripped back more recent layers, last month they came across some wonderful 18th century painted panels. These dated to a hundred years or more after the keep was last rebuilt, and the now deteriorating battlements installed. The discovery had necessitated a change in plans. And now this disaster. How utterly horrible - that poor woman.

The morning was spent being bossed around by local council officials and the police. By early afternoon, the site was secured with high-visibility barriers and bright yellow crime-scene tape. Pratt wrote up an emergency application for authorisation and funds to secure the castle battlements and undertake a survey of necessary repairs. A proper risk and safety assessment would be required, for the whole castle.

The keep which Pratt's team had been exploring was just below the damaged roof sections which had fallen on poor Sheila - one of the oldest parts of the castle. Mention of the keep was curiously sparse in the London Chancellery archives.

Pratt assured his team that anyone too shocked by the horrific accident need not come in to work for the time being. Anyway, the authorities and castle management had told them to stop work for now. Tomorrow, Pratt and a couple of volunteers would mothball the project. He had explained to the police that they couldn't just drop everything, on such a delicate operation. Some packing up and putting away was needed. Hopefully, this would be just a temporary interruption. They were all keen to examine the great fireplace and mysterious panels.

...

The next day, Professor Pratt departed for the castle before sunrise, leaving Natalie and the kids asleep at home in Edmonton. He turned on Radio 4 driving through Epping Forest, catching a brief mention of Sheila's death. Nothing about the university. Good.

Sunrise on dappled leaves - glimpse of a fox-tail, darting into the undergrowth.

He turned down the long gravel drive to Broglin Castle with its famous beech tree rows. Pratt drove through tall shadows and shafts of sunlight. In the near distance, looming battlements and turrets silhouetted against the dawn.

Pratt was earlier than expected, so he had breakfast (continental) at the famous Broglin Pantry. He sloshed down a second cup of weak coffee, then out through the dining-room side door, and round the croquet lawn to an ancient doorway into the old castle keep.

As he keyed the touchpad, Pratt noticed a huge black bat wheeling beneath branches, on the edge of his vision off to the left.

"Late out for a bat. And a big one."

After pulling back the five hundred year-old oak and iron door, he slipped past the flimsy stairwell cordon. Then up three flights of steep stone stairs to the upper chamber. Prof. Pratt paused near the top on a small landing, glad to notice that - unlike six weeks ago - he was not out of breath.

Up a few more steps and into the 'master suite' (as they semi-jokingly called it). Maggie and Jasper Peters were already there.

His postgraduate students were snogging. Pratt would have to remember to knock next time.

"Euch – disgusting! Newlyweds!"

"Yeah, yeah" - a disengaging Jasper - "I told you we should get a room."

"Right - on Pratt's pittance! Chance would be a fine thing" – his wife of one month.

Pratt smiled indulgently - "Well – you two don't seem too perturbed by yesterday's events."

This took the fun out of the room.

"Bad choice of words. Sorry."

"I told you so", said Maggie - obviously cross.

"Our first row - thanks Prof", said Jasper.

"Come on - as we're here, down to work.

Let's have a look at that plaster and the wallpaper around the mantle before Gerald gets here."

Dr Osguard was due in later that morning to inspect the recently revealed interiors, still seemingly intact under centuries of paper and whitewash.

"Fortunate he's due in today."

The three of them stared at a double row of green-glazed tiles, which Gerald had last week pronounced "gorgeous". This had put the mantelpiece itself temporarily out of bounds, but did not preclude more digging around the stone uprights, ten feet apart on either side of the great hearth.

"These huge slabs are solid. Must have been a challenge, winching them up here - presumably?"

"You know Jasper, that would make an excellent dissertation. I think

Geoff Taylor at Queens would be interested in a question like that. You should keep it in mind for one of the grad-students.

But I don't think this place is typical. As Sally was saying, it seems there's a fair amount of brickwork between these rooms and the upper fortifications, but no further chambers as such. Or at least, nothing obvious. Seems like wasted space."

Pointing to the ceiling - "When we get back on the roof, we should do a Carling scan. I wonder if there might be something else up there, overlooked or walled over?

... but that will have to wait for another day.

Really - it's too bad."

Pratt cleared his throat.

While the Peters poked, Pratt peered down through the lead-laced glass of the high turret window, overlooking the pathway. He could make out a large dark stain on the gravel far below, distorted through the thick glass.

Half an hour later, not much progress had been made when Sally arrived.

They had a lot to do today.

"Sally – we need to ask the manager again for access to the back records - or whatever they call them. He said there was a lot of material in the hotel annex, somewhere in the basement - right? It's ridiculous - almost the most up-to-date information we have is from a tourist guidebook."

"Yes boss."

"But not today. The poor chap will be busy enough as it is.

If that doesn't work, I'll make a formal application to the company. Chasing the historical paper trail can wait for now."

"Yes boss."

Most of the furniture had been removed many years ago - some of it more recently to the newer annex. All except the big bed and a couple of large empty trunks, of uncertain provenance.

And here was Gerald - punctual and punctilious.

"Good morning everyone."

A quarter-hour later, Pratt and the Peters stood slightly back from

Dr Osguard, as he talked them through scenes of hunting, minor deities and nymphs.

"Thanks so much, Peter. These are really excellent. Not particularly rare, but fine examples. Notice Adonis' torso. Lovely.

I'll need an hour or so to get my photos and make some notes.

Really, these deserve proper looking after. Anything in the budget for that?"

"Not that I'm aware, Gerald.

But you know - Staymore Hotels will need a conservator. After yesterday, they'll have to take this place more seriously. I will be recommending a proper safety assessment, and a full architectural and archaeological survey. Including these panels, of course.

They'll have to make a substantial intervention, if this place isn't going to fall apart and cause more damage." He thumped the ancient stone walls.

"Careful Peter – you'll bring the whole place down!"

The others tittered politely. Someone seems to make this joke every day. Not appropriate really, in the circumstances.

There was a faint rumble from somewhere above.

Frowning, Gerald continued - "Broglin Castle - seat of the Counts Cornich.

You know, that would make a much better draw than the present slogan. What is it – 'A night of cut glass and Gothic'? A bit trashy, if you ask me.

But this chamber would have been quite sumptuous in its prime, for the time. Much nicer than that dreary late Victoriana" - a condescending sweep of his long nose towards the hotel wing, seen below through large bay windows in the adjoining room.

This drew the little group's attention to some activity on the pathway below. Policemen bustling in and out of a blue tent stationed near the recently blood-soaked stones and gravel.

"Poor woman." Maggie had been quiet for a while.

A radio played pop tunes, muffled in the distance.

Then - a huge crash, from directly above.

Pratt was nearest the window. He stood back instinctively, then half-opened the window and looked down. A policeman was looking up.

"Someone on the roof, sir - one of ours. Just a stumble - he's all right now."

Louder - "Denton! Be careful up there. Watch your footing! We don't want another disaster, you idiot."

A muted response from above, among the battlements.

Pratt and colleagues returned to the panels. Osguard stepped a little closer, then back again.

"There's something rather special about this group of figures, you know. Look at that chap staring into the pond. I thought at first it was Narcissus, gazing fondly at his reflection. Maybe that's it - but look at those eyes.

Surprised I didn't notice before."

Despite the faded paint, the tiny figure's eyes burned with golden intensity. He somehow appeared both radiant and sickly.

Peering more closely at the tiny figures, both men saw something else, emerging from the painted reeds and shrubs behind the green and golden youth. A larger looming figure, also with dimly glowing eyes - something strange and sickening scarlet about the mouth. A shiver went down Pratt's spine.

He was about to say something -

Another huge crash from above, followed split-seconds later by a wrenching sound – which intensified into a rush of collapsing brick, dirty air and rubble. The leaded windowpane shattered - the room filled with dust.

Jake let out a shriek. He staggered back into his wife - both fell sitting to the floor.

The room was almost silent for a moment. Jake and Maggie Peters exchanged shocked glances, then looked up to where Pratt and Osguard stood back to the left. Dust allover settling on their clothes and heads.

Then another loud echoing creak, and more dust. Something massive moving quickly.

A scream quickly broken off with another crashing sound - something massive exploding into the chamber through the wall. Then blood everywhere - splattered across the walls - twirling motes of crimson dust.

Something huge and dark and ancient had smashed through the

panels, and down into the middle of the room. Encountering Mr and Mrs Peters, it had destroyed their upper bodies, now oozing beneath the dark grey stone.

Pratt didn't notice that he was lightly flecked in blood. He rubbed his eyes, reopened them - was presented with a ten-foot by five-foot by five-foot stone-slabbed block.

A huge coffin - or so it seemed, amid the bloody dust and smell of rot and sulphur.

Protruding from beneath, four legs.

Osguard had fainted. Feeling wobbly himself, Pratt sunk to the ground. Sally stood staring open-mouthed.

...

The police again. More terrible than yesterday. The coffin had to be moved. It was a piece of evidence, as well as being of historic importance. It would be impossible to know what - if anything - was inside, without scanning and careful unpacking, which "couldn't be done in an attic", as Constable Denton pointed out.

Three days later the coffin was manoeuvred by a police forensics team, the fire brigade, local council authorities and a group of volunteers from London University, on ingenious levers out through the bay windows, and lowered to the ground below. Two weeks later, the upper tower partially collapsed, destroying the bed in which an Archbishop's bastard and a prince had once slept (separated by a century).

The giant coffin rested a few hours beneath the battlements, near the site of the earlier incident. Nearby on old stone walls and drainpipes, a dirty black mildew began to spread. Petunias in the flowerbeds wilted.

It was late afternoon by the time the lifting device and flatbed truck to take the coffin into central London had set up. A localised stink of decay and pestilence was apparent to anyone who walked by. After the coffin was removed the smell receded, but did not dissipate entirely for many days.

Driving back into London through Epping Forest, the flatbed truck overheated. Something to do with the water-pump.

It was past 11 o'clock by the time the coffin was unloaded at

Ladbroke College and shifted to a secure storage room at the back of the courtyard.

The Vice Chancellor had told Pratt to stay home for a few days. Of course, the accident was not his fault, but the poor fellow should rest.

Responsibilities for this stage of the operation fell to the porters. Given the significance of recent events, and of the consignment arriving from Epping, unloading and storage would be overseen by Prof Gordon Grim, Reader in Esoteric Studies. Sally kept him company, out of loyalty to Pratt and the department. A police officer had checked in at ten, to ascertain progress.

Not long afterwards, someone claiming to be a journalist had knocked on the porters' office door, asking about the coffin and its contents. Geoff the security guard didn't like the look of him. Seemed weirdly agitated, and shifty-eyed.

Across the courtyard in the old common room, Grim and Sally were drinking coffee and distractedly discussing a new book on *The Eastern Occult* (Sally liked it, Grim didn't), when the head porter popped his head into the room – "Consignment secured."

Still annoyed at the call on his time, but pleased to see Pratt in trouble, Grim checked his phone while Geoff locked up for the night. Then, with a perfunctory - "Thank you Sally, good night" - and a curt nod to the head porter, he walked back across the courtyard to the staff car park, thoughts on the mysterious package they would begin to unwrap in the morning.

Switching on the Tesla and Radio 4, he pulled out too quickly - and nearly ran down Nancy, as she rounded the corner heading out of the staff entrance at the back of the main building. Winding down the window, Grim muttered "sorry".

Nancy didn't have a chance to say "no problem" (or was it "never mind"?), as he sped off. Pleased to be done with work - for tonight at least - she unlocked her bicycle, and headed to Tattenham.

It had been a trying few days. Nancy listened to the BBC News most mornings before heading to work. No mention of a murder in Mayfair - no policeman knocking on her door.

Surely you couldn't just kill someone - even a vampire - and get away with it? Surely it was just a matter of time?

It didn't occur to Nancy that the vampires might come after her.

...

Later that night a bat circled the Ladbroke College courtyard, glimmering beneath the security lights. A dog barked - a motorbike revved in the street outside. Somewhere in the distance, someone was shouting.

Then silence save a far-off siren.

Geoff stepped out of the cubicle to smoke. He caught a glimpse of someone or thing loitering in the shadows at the end of the street. A trick of the light?

Then - a deep grating sound from the storage shed, at the back of the university compound. It stopped, then resumed - followed by a very loud thud.

What the heck was that?

Back in the cubicle, there was nothing on the screens. He had better go and investigate. That Grim could be a nasty piece of work. Best not to give him any reason for complaint.

A putrid stink pervaded the courtyard – most revolting towards the back where the storerooms were. Geoff could hear something moving back there.

The security guard's body was never found.

'Mystery of The Empty Coffin', the papers called it.

...

A few weeks later, the Pratts had new dinner guests. Peter had told Natalie about the remarkable young woman who did cleaning at the department.

"Well - if she is so bright and interested, why don't you ask this Nancy over for dinner? Always good to meet new people.

And after all that nastiness at work, it will be nice to talk about something different."

Pratt asked Nancy if she would like to bring a companion, so Saw Wah came along too. She introduced him as her friend from Burma, and also from church. Like Nancy, he was a refugee.

Natalie Pratt liked them at once.

"Just a friend perhaps - for now. But did you see how they were sitting? A hair's breadth between their hands on the dinner table.

And they suit each other, don't you think."

As usual, Mrs Pratt was right.

Chapter 2

It is one year later - 2023. Nancy and Saw Wah are two months married.

His village back home in Burma has moved a few times over the years – fleeing conflict, and to cultivate new rice fields in the Papun hills. Saw Wah's family – or some of them – live 150 miles northeast of the many-roomed, ramshackle house in a suburb to the north of Yangon, where Nancy grew up. Her family spoke Sgaw Karen and a bit of English at home, Burmese in school and the market, and when engaging with government authorities. Saw Wah spoke nothing but Karen and a smattering of Thai before arriving in England.

Before leaving Yangon in terror and anger 13 years ago, Nancy had only been in the Karen State of southeast Burma twice, as a child visiting relatives with her parents. Dark hardwood floors, worn smooth and cool. Huge tropical palm trees in the courtyard. Baby bears in a cage – such sharp and playful claws. She remembered a loom for weaving - playing with the coloured threads ... Leaf-thatch bamboo huts, emerald rice fields. Enormous, dirty buffaloes and little fishies in clear cool streams.

Nancy had been a star pupil in school. Then, as an 18-year-old university student (physics major), she had been part of a bungled operation and had to get out of town quickly. Looking back, they had been crazy. Three of her comrades had been killed, two under torture. Nancy had been lucky to escape with her life - up into the conflict zone where the Karen National Union battled the Myanmar Army.

Two years later (with Nancy by then in the UK, in hospital) the KNU agreed a ceasefire with the then semi-civilian Myanmar government. For a few years, there was relative peace across much of Burma - although the Myanmar Army launched fresh attacks against Kachin civilians and rebels in the north. The uneasy KNU ceasefire fell apart on 1 February 2021, when the military took over the country again, unleashing hell on the population. Hundreds of thousands of people took to the streets; many took up arms against the hated junta, including some of Nancy's old friends. This past 18 months she had been raising money for them as best she could, together with Saw Wah and the Karen community in London.

A new wave of 'Gen Z' democracy activists and fighters from the towns and cities had joined the battle-hardened ethnic rebels up in the hills. For the first time in decades, Myanmar's multitude of insurgent groups were on the front foot - taking the battle to the enemy and scoring a string of victories. The territory of Kawthoolei, the Karen rebel state, had expanded back into areas which the KNU had not controlled since the 1950s. The Kachin and other ethnic armed groups in the north were also on the offensive, fighting for democracy and self-determination. But the junta was battling desperately, attacking civilians and insurgents indiscriminately by land and air.

The airstrikes were a terrifying new development – Russian-supplied jet bombers and high-impact explosives. Nancy had never experienced such a thing.

Thirteen years ago she had fled into the war-zone, travelling incognito by bus and then on foot, up into the hills of Kawthoolei. In doing so, Nancy was returning to a homeland she had never really known. Safe, at least temporarily, among her own people - but also a visitor from the cities.

The KNU had been battling successive military regimes for independence for the best part of a century. They had established an under-resourced but resilient government system in liberated areas along the Thailand border, including health and education services for civilians, and an effective but overstretched relief system.

For a year Nancy made herself useful, teaching in a KNU high-school behind the front lines. After that she worked briefly in the KNU administration.

And then the ambush. It had been hushed up, on the eve of the cease-fire. The KNU got Nancy out to safety in Thailand, and the UK did the right thing - granting her asylum and access to medical treatment. Many others had not been so fortunate, she knew.

Nancy was lucky not to have died. Now she was okay, mostly.

Saw Wah's father had been a KNU soldier, his mother killed by the

Burmese military. A brother and a sister were still in Thailand, long-term refugees; two more brothers were working on Thai fishing boats. He has not heard from them in years. He believes at least one of them to be dead.

Saw Wah would tell her stories, with photos of beautiful Dhawlu Township in the hills above Papun town. Many of his cousins, aunts and uncles had been killed, or fled - as far as the USA. Others stayed on in Kawthoolei. One day he would return - and she with him.

...

Nancy was determined to put the strange incidents recounted above behind her. Just as she had after the fantastical events at Frogmort Manor, three years ago.

She was surprised and relieved that there had been no consequences to killing the vampire - so far. She thanked God, and tried not to think about it too much. That seemed to have worked last time.

She asked Saw Wah once or twice what he thinks about vampires, but he turned it into a joke. She mostly keeps the trembling in her heart out of her voice when she speaks to him about this.

Saw Wah is not much interested in western ghouls - but he knows about the De Breh. The Karen spirit-monster of springs in the rocks above creeks. Long, shaggy white hair, hanging like strips of noodle. Scary children's stories - but like her, he is not sure of the reality. Probably not the sort of thing Christians should believe in? But then again, this is their cultural heritage.

"And the De Breh is not evil, Nancy.

He is a spirit - very close to our people in the hills. For generations and generations. Like a guardian.

He doesn't accept any sacrifices. Not like those Nat spirits.

But not many people see him these days. Not like in the past, when the grandparents used to spot him in the forest, or up among the rocks. I think he's been frightened away by the war - and by the church as well, I suppose.

When I was little, the old people used to talk about them. Not so much these days, I think."

"Maybe it's climate change", said Nancy.

Nancy and Saw Wah are helping people back in Burma fight against the dictator, and the struggle for a just and free Kawthoolei. Now they are married, both feel able to do more for those back home, and the revolution. Together with other Burmese exiles, they protest and raise funds. Once a month they stand with a small group outside the junta representative office in central London, chanting against the dictators.

One day they learned that a close relative of Saw Wah had been captured by the Myanmar Army, tortured and killed. Her husband said he wasn't bitter or angry, which Nancy understands - but he was sad, and had a thirst for justice. For them, righteous anger was different to the personal kind.

Several years ago Nancy had taken another, mostly unpaid part-time job. BurmaAction is a small outfit, where a dozen or so Karen and other Burmese activists work side-by-side with a handful of British volunteers; mostly young Londoners, and a few kindly older people. She started doing translations between Karen, English and Burmese. Now Nancy does much of the admin work. They advocate for the cause, and raise funds for refugees and internally displaced villagers. Saw Wah helps out sometimes at BurmaAction, when he's not busy with the carpentry.

Auntie May had been right about her marrying Saw Wah - "Such a handsome, pleasant and reliable young man." And she had been right to encourage Nancy in getting back to the Burma struggle. Auntie herself was very quiet and gentle, and religious. She sometimes listened to Nancy's dreams. But Nancy never told her about the vampire, or the strange glowing rubies.

Instead of gunshots and shouting, last night Nancy had dreamt again of the exquisite jade dragon, and also of the glowing purple lights. The images remained, long after other cobwebs dissolved. This must be connected to the incident with the vampire.

Still nothing on the news, no knock on the door. Best not to think about it. She had had enough fear and bloodshed in her life already.

But still there was the leather-bound notebook. She had placed this carefully beneath her "unmentionables" (she liked the English word) - presumably safe beyond even beloved Saw Wah's enquiries. She had almost mentioned it to him last night, but then he said something about "let sleeping dogs lie" - trying out a new English phrase.

Nancy very much did not believe in omens, but did believe that sometimes God gives people a nudge in the right direction. Saw Wah's reaction suggested she should keep on keeping the encounter with Silk to herself, and likewise the notebook, and the white tiger (the cool marble tiger).

...

It was pouring down when Nancy woke at dawn, and had been raining for much of the night. Difficult enough cycling to work; almost impossible coming back, with water hip-deep in places around the university. She had to leave her bike in the sheds at work and walk a mile or more through flooded streets before she could find a bus still running to Tattenham. Dead rats floating in the gutters, grey water washing over the thresholds of shops, offices, and down into tube stations. In odd moments like this she felt herself back in Yangon, in the intense rains. London was just as gloomy, if not more. Almost as dirty on days like this, and much colder!

Nancy was grimy and shivering by the time she got home. After showering, she changed into a fresh tamein, wrapping the colourful cotton shaft around herself. She boiled water for a cup of jasmine tea - not much liking the milky English stuff.

Conscious of prevarication, she spent some time on her phone, catching up on the parlous state of her homeland. In the two years since the coup, the Karen and other freedom fighters had made significant advances – although the cost and suffering had been immense.

Meanwhile, in the lowlands a shifting network of anti-coup fighters continued to badger and harass the Myanmar Army, making it more difficult for the enemy to focus their dwindling forces. Poorly trained and mostly lightly armed, but hugely committed and brave, an army of young people were paying with their lives to hold back - and in some places, push back - the tide of violence. Beheadings were common - on both sides, mostly by the military and their lackeys.

Despite assaults by land and air, young pro-democracy fighters still held a few bases in the dry central plains. Their fighting skills had improved - as well as the supply and local production of weapons and ammunition. But the bulk of liberated areas were still in the Karen, Karenni, Chin, Kachin, Ta'ang and northern Shan State hills. This horseshoe of mountain and border states, surrounding the Burman-populated lowlands, had long been the hold-out of ethnic armed groups struggling for autonomy. But now the rebels were moving down into the valleys.

This year her cousin in the Karen State capital Pa'an messaged her that the rains were more irregular and intense. Each year, the flooding was worse, up and down the country. A little more rain was falling - but in a shorter and more unpredictable rainy season. This and the searing temperatures were playing havoc with the rice harvest. Combined with rising sea levels and salination in many low-lying, rice producing areas, crops were in danger of failing. The situation was a little better in the less densely populated uplands, but not much.

By Nancy's calculation, these days the junta (never "government") and a patchwork of ethnic insurgents and pro-democracy fighters controlled about a third of the country each – the rebels maybe a bit more, with the rest "contested" - subject to violent attacks by the Myanmar Army, and guerrilla assaults by anti-coup forces. The enemy still sometimes rained death from the air - although less so than before, since the junta began running low on air-fuel, and the opposition gained access to a few anti-aircraft missiles.

...

Saw Wah's family wrote to them from the Thailand border refugee camps - "Are you coming back?" "We thought you had forgotten us."

Old comrades messaged Nancy, from Amsterdam and Indiana, from Chiang Mai.

Cousin (now KNU Lt.Col.) Philip sent greetings from Papun. This small town in northern Karen State was once and now again headquarters of the KNU - capital of Kawthoolei.

Nancy sighed, and turned again to the notebook. Only the second time she had done so since that evening.

White Tiger, Green Dragon.

She picked up the smooth white statuette, turning it over in her hands.

There were a few more lines in English scattered through the notebook. Most of it was written in what she had decided (correctly) was Latin.

Soon - soon, soon.

On the last page, in newer ink -

She doesn't know.
She doesn't know!

Other English language inclusions were place names, some of them in London (Highgate, Epping, Bloomsbury, Mayfair), a few in Europe (she recognised Paris and Pompeii), or Thailand and Burma (Chiang Mai and Bangkok, Rangoon and Papun.)

A few phrases she recognised as Pali - the language of Theravada Buddhism. As a Christian, she was not familiar with these, but they didn't seem particularly Buddhist.

A few other place names in Burmese – including the Three Pagodas Pass, to the south of Papun on the Thailand border.

And again –

Beneath the Burmese Bell.

This was getting too close to home again. Nancy closed the notebook, annoyed that she had broken her rule. She had put this behind her.

But yesterday's visit to Ratcliffe Gardens had spooked her. And now her head was aching terribly.

...

Nancy and the Count

Yesterday after church, Nancy and Saw Wah had taken the bus to Ratcliffe Gardens. Fine gentle late afternoon sun. They drank green tea from a flask and ate ice creams. Towards evening, before getting back on the bus, they had taken a circuit through the western end of the gardens, which were more unkempt with some big trees and patches of uncut grass.

The garden was not crowded, even among the ornamental flower-beds. Here among the willows and other trees they could not name, there were almost no other people - occasional snatches of laughter or children shrieking in the distance. Hand in hand, they walked slowly along a partly overgrown path. Smell of nectar and buzz of bees.

It occurred to Nancy that she was happier now than at any time since arriving in England. There had been ferocious joys and searing terrors during her time on the streets of Yangon, and later in the jungle - very different to this delight. Enjoy the moment, Nancy.

A change in the light through the branches ahead. Languidly, they followed the path into a tree-lined clearing - to be presented by a Burmese bell, suspended in mid-air.

There was no mistaking it. Three feet high, 18 inches at the base, cast in bronze (presumably) and much weathered. Hanging from a high oak branch.

"A Burmese bell" she exclaimed, dumbly.

"A Burmese bell."

And what is more, she knew this bell. From a dream? A memory?

"It is a bell.

Is it Burmese?

Presumably my darling, there are other kinds?"

"Let's see, my dear." Saw Wah heard the trembling in her voice.

From below, it was difficult to make out much. One could presumably strike the bell with a stick. However, it was too high to be reached otherwise - even by someone taller than them.

There was a better view from the edge of the small clearing.

A sizeable metal bell, hanging from a thick branch. Nancy had no doubt it was from Burma. She was sure she had seen it before.

The shifting sunlight revealed faint markings. Nancy shivered - fear, anticipation, something else – a memory just below the surface.

"We had better get moving, or we'll miss the bus - come on."

Saw Wah could tell that something had changed, because of the bell. One of the reasons that she loved him was his lack of - not curiosity, but he knew when not to push things. Saw Wah never asked her to reveal more than she wanted to.

They sat mostly in silence on the way home. She read her Bible; he checked his phone. Arsenal were on for the double!

...

That evening she told Saw Wah everything, at the nice Indian cafe round the corner from their newly shared flat. She should have done this before they got married - she knew that now.

Saw Wah didn't say much afterwards - except "I believe you".

They looked together through the notebook, but couldn't find anything more about the bell. Something about Michelangelo - whom they knew to be a great and dead Italian artist - but most of that was in Latin. Some more Pali magical formula (or at least, that's what Saw Wah thinks).

In two night's time, they would return to Ratcliffe Gardens. They considered but rejected asking permission. They would need torches and a step-ladder, and some means of transport better than bus, bicycle or Uber.

In the meantime, Nancy and Saw Wah did some sleuthing. Wikipedia revealed that Broglin Castle had been acquired by the nation after World War Two. Then sold to private investors in the 1990s.

As far as Nancy could remember, this was indeed the place in Silk's photos. Eventually, she decided to ask Professor Pratt about it, as casually as she could.

Important artifacts had been destroyed when the tower collapsed - "But that was hardly the greatest disaster on that terrible day."

He paused.

"The last Count Cornich disappeared sometime in the mid-19th century, childless.

He spent some time in Burma, you know. Your country, Nancy.

Thus your interest, I suppose ..."

No reply from Nancy.

"He was out there running timber extraction and export, mostly teak. That was one source of the family's money. Also slaves and precious stones. The Corniches were old money – from way back, at least to the 17th century. They seem to have had some odd relationships with the old Thai kingdom of Ayutthaya.

The Cornich line dies out a couple of centuries later. Last seen in Lisbon in the late 1850s.

The last Count's grandfather was a Colonel in British India and Burma in the 1820s and '30s. He fought in the first Anglo-Burmese War, you know. But there's not much in the records on that either.

Very curious."

...

On schedule at 9pm Saw Wah picked her up in a hatchback borrowed from work. They had to park close to the Southgate walls, in order not to attract attention with the ladder. The perimeter fence gave way to a low-ish hedge at this relatively secluded point.

They drank tea from a thermos flask sitting in the car, and reviewed the plan. The hedge was not as low as Nancy had remembered, but it was not too much trouble getting the ladder and themselves over it, and into the secluded grove.

The bell was hanging in moonlight.

They prayed, then set up the stepladder. Nancy held on, while Saw Wah ascended.

The moon was bright and full. Saw Wah shaded his brow, as if to look into the distance.

"I can see our flat from up here!"

"No you can't, silly man - no way you can see Tattenham from there." She frowned up as he smiled down - then she smiled up as he frowned down.

"Are you quite steady, my dear?" - "Yes, I think so."

She handed up a large sheet of paper, then a carton of crayons they had bought that afternoon.

"Thank you darling. This is not going to be easy".

Twenty minutes later he had worked up a sweat, which hadn't helped. Working by headtorch and moonlight, Saw Wah had produced three sheets of blotchy paper rubbings, covering much of the bell's inscribed surface.

"Come on, my dear.

Let's get moving, before someone spots us."

Nancy helped him down, then put the damp sheaves in her backpack.

She collapsed the stepladder.

Saw Wah was crouching, directly beneath the bell.

"It did say - 'beneath the Burmese bell' - didn't it?"

"It did."

"Not - 'on the Burmese bell' - right?"

"Correct."

"Well - I can't see anything here."

The ground was hard-packed, with some bald patches in the otherwise lush grass - probably where people had stood to admire the bell, or maybe strike it.

"Any sign of digging?"

There wasn't.

"Come on, let's go."

...

Back at the apartment after dropping off the car, they made tea, and prayed for guidance and protection, and pain relief. Little lumps of long-gone phantom shrapnel tore at her temple.

Focus on something else. On the rubbings - which did not reveal much.

The inscriptions seemed to be a mixture of Pali and Burmese, most of it unreadable. The condition of the bell, Saw Wah's inexpert work, their poor scholarship. One short passage might identify a patron monarch, a partially obscured list of religious terms.

"There's not much here."

"A dead end".

They sat for a while in silence. Then - "More tea, my dear?

What next?"

"Let's try the internet again."

They searched again for Ratcliffe Gardens.

They knew already that the gardens dated from the seventeen-hundreds - much re-developed in the late-19th century. They had once belonged to some great dynasty.

"Hang on my dear - there's a link to the historic parks department."

More tea-leaf salad.

"I've got an email address."

...

Meanwhile, to the southwest beyond the other side of London, two large transit vans pulled into an almost deserted car-park at the foot of Box Hill. The same make, one was disguised as a plumber's mobile unit, the other plain grey.

After switching off engines, both vehicles sat silent for a moment before two large men got down from the grey front cab. There was a muffled sound from the back of the van. The larger man slammed his fist into the side panels.

"Shut up!

Keep it quiet, or I'll rip your head off."

There was one other vehicle at the rear of the car-park - a large black SUV with tinted windows, partially obscured under the night shadows of large trees. Two figures emerge and proceed slowly towards the new arrivals.

The bulky one in front moves with a slight limp, his features obscured by the night and a wide-brimmed hat. A few steps behind him, a taller figure looms and shimmers. Both are dressed mostly in black – but only the Count seems to suck the night into him. He hangs back in the shadows of the moon, while the man in front steps forward.

"Detective-Sargent Jikes."

"I told you before - no names.

What have you got?"

The driver of the grey van is doing the talking. The other has unbuttoned his jacket, revealing a pistol stuck in his waistband.

"Just in case - just in case."

"Hmphh" – the Familiar looks over his shoulder, communicating in silence with the Count, still in the shadows. He returns his attention to the traffickers. A cock of the eyebrows.

Gun man shifts uneasily. He is not used to being intimidated, and is not sure how Jikes – or the figure in the shadows – is doing it. He shivered involuntarily.

"Right then – let's get on with it.

There's six in the back of each van. Take your pick.

Mostly from Syria, as far as we can tell. Couple of Dolomenes.

Shouldn't be any complications. No paperwork."

"Alright - let's have a look." Gun man unlocked the back of the vans.

...

Twenty minutes and £70,000 later, the three vehicles depart in separate directions.

The Count is pleased with his selection. Three young men for the Marylebone Street basement; a variety of blood types. The present incumbents are drained to the dregs - manacles no longer necessary, beyond the prevention of self-harm.

They will be given to Jikes for messy dungeon play.

The three new men are strong - should last a while. Discreet nutrition.

"Jikes - get them to eat and drink a little. Impress on them that the ordeal will not be short, so they should fortify themselves.

Greatly improves the taste.

Impress on them quite sternly. If necessary, you may make an example of the smaller one - in which case I will observe.

I know you like to take their eyes. That should encourage les autres.

Of course, lots of fresh vegetables. Also feed them some oats."

The other two slaves - the women - would meet more complicated fates. Selected for the hunt. Jikes and his team would set them up with 'jobs' - probably something to do with the nightclub, or perhaps the road haulage company. Over the next few weeks, the Count will have his fun.

First some nocturnal visits and stalking. To make this part enjoyable, it was important that the victims thought they had found new lives in England - secure and not too onerous. This would make their eventual despair more complete, more delicious. He would lure them into momentary comfort, even hope. Perhaps half-decent accommodation through a not too bad job - or even just the promise. Then rip it all away, dragging out old traumas - before revealing the full terror. Their worst fears would pale in comparison with his appetites. They called it 'vampire romance'. Fun and games, then feasting on her ripped-out throat.

Fangs flashing horribly, the Count licked his lips.

...

The parks office replied two days later, while Nancy and Saw Wah were having breakfast. It was disappointing news, at first. They were unable to help with the enquiry regarding Ratcliffe Gardens.

Twenty minutes later though, a second email: should they be interested, records and artefacts from the previous owners had been deposited with the British Museum in the 1950s, and earlier.

These include some etchings from the later 19th Century, one or more of which may feature an image of the bell. I trust that this information will help in your enquiries.

So - a clue after all.

There was no reply to their further emails, asking for details or advice. Could they just walk into the British Museum and ask to see these etchings? They would need more than a ladder. Nancy thought she might know someone who could help.

...

From a couple of brief conversations in corridors at the university, Nancy knew Sally Weston to be friendly – and indeed she was happy to help. Nancy had an air about her which made you want to lend a hand.

They met in the cafeteria after Nancy's shift. Sally didn't tell Nancy she had stayed behind two hours after work. Under the strip-lighting, Nancy looked tired.

"A Burmese bell at Ratcliffe Gardens? How curious" - although why she was so curious, Sally couldn't tell.

Of course she would help to track down the etchings. Sally would pop into the museum tomorrow - or latest, the day after.

"That's so kind of you Sally. I didn't know who else to ask."

"You are very welcome Nancy.

I'll ask Tom Scott in Indian antiquities. He helped me with the PhD - sort of an informal adviser. Nice guy. Doctorate from Aberdeen.

You said that you've told Peter about your interests.

You might want to mention this little quest to him. But up to you."

"I will Sally - but not quite yet.

It's just a private thing of mine, and I don't want to bother him. After all, I'm only a cleaner."

She had almost forgotten. Nancy was more inquisitive and resourceful than many of the undergraduates Sally taught.

"Did you know that what's on display at the BM is only about 5% of the museum's entire collection?

What you are looking for is probably down in the store-rooms - or else somewhere off-site. They have warehouses south of the river, and in Essex. Anyway, I'll try to find out."

She smiles and sips her tea.

"Shall I tell Tom you are doing a bit of private research - because of the connection to Burma?"

"Yes - please do that."

They talked a bit about Nancy's life in England - the many operations on her legs. Their shared love of volley-ball. Nancy was patient and polite, but Sally could tell that she needed to be away.

...

The following week, Nancy and Saw Wah met Sally after lunch on the British Museum back steps, across Rutland Square from the university.

"Right then – this way."

First, she showed them the Burmese display cases on the ground floor.

"Adjacent to the much more extensive Indian collections - like Burma's relationship to India, under the Raj."

A joke?

An elegantly carved wooden Buddha image from the early Pagan era - very rare, apparently. Undeniably beautiful. Green-glazed terra-cotta plaques from the base of the great Shwemadaw Pagoda in Pegu, depicting the army of Mara –

"Who tried to distract the Buddha at the point of enlightenment. See how the Naga earth spirit raises seven heads above the Lord Buddha, shielding him from Mara's soldiers, and from the seduction of the tempter's dancing daughters."

Interesting – but nothing much relevant to her quest.

"Fear not - this way.

"To Tom's cubbyhole."

...

Tom Scott thought what they sought was probably 'downstairs'.

"This will be a good test of the old systems. Pre-digital.

Lucky for you I owe the Professor a favour."

Nancy made a mental note: did Sally tell Pratt?

Also - there was something familiar about Tom.

They were sitting in his cramped office, tucked behind one of the main stairwells - perched on stools in front of Tom's leather-topped desk, on which were spread piles of old ledgers. To Sally and Tom, the scene was pleasingly Dickensian – wood-panelled walls, weak sunlight through an upper window, old furniture and cups of tea. To Nancy and Saw Wah, the cubbyhole looked like a Burmese civil service office. Nancy sipped the milky tea; Saw Wah did not. But he ate the biscuits.

The next twenty minutes dragged a bit.

"Well - that's 1951 through '52."

Tom handed another vast portfolio across the table. Sally started working through the delicate pages.

"What exquisite penmanship."

Nancy and Saw Wah sat either side of Sally. Tom indicated a pile of three hardback notebooks.

"These are - or they should be – contemporary records of privately donated prints and other 'non-manuscripts, non-paintings' from the respective years" - he taps the pile.

"People - we are looking for entries mentioning Ratcliffe Gardens, or a Burmese bell ... and/or - anything else?" Looking at Nancy.

"Papun, Burma.

Or any mention of Roger Silk."

"Roger Silk, eh? Who's that Nancy?"

"Oh - just someone I ran into.

His family could be connected to the bell."

Saw Wah shot his wife a sideways glance. They had agreed not to mention the vampire. Which technically she hadn't.

The others didn't seem to have noticed.

Now Nancy knew where she had seen Tom before – at Frogmort Manor. He had been staying as a guest, at one of their spooky symposiums. Nancy had mostly been invisible, as part of the domestic staff. Not surprising he didn't recognise her. She would say nothing. That was a can of worms for another day.

The search turned up no leads. Sally and Tom had to be getting back to work.

"Tell you what: come back at five - or better make it five-thirty. We can have a dig around downstairs. That will be fun - just for half an hour.

I'm thinking of those stacks next to the Calcutta archives?" – too himself - "The old Burma ledgers are supposed to be in better nick."

Looking at Nancy - "Can't promise anything, of course - but I like it down there. Don't mind taking a look, if you have the time."

Of course they did.

In the meantime, Nancy and Saw Wah took up Tom's suggestion to explore "the best museum in the world".

They shared a KitKat, a custard tart and an apple in the vast white stone rotunda.

"That's the most expensive fruit I've ever eaten!"

Good job they had bought sandwiches.

"Where first my dear?"

Out of respect to the land which had taken them in, they headed to first to Viking England. Swords and rusted shields – an air of sacred violence. An extraordinary golden mask.

"But I think they became more gentle, after they were Christians."

"Possibly."

"Nancy – do you remember that nice Norwegian man who visited a few months back at BurmaAction? He was a Christian, as he often mentioned. And a very nice man. See what a little loving-kindness does."

Saw Wah wanted to see the mummies, for which the British Museum was famous. Nancy was less keen. They would have a look, anyway.

"We don't have to, of course. It's already past five." He wouldn't ask her to wait alone for him, not in a spooky place like this.

"That's okay - I can sit here."

Nancy sat on a bench outside the Egyptian rooms, trying to get something useful out of the book on English country houses she had bought in the gift shop. Although it didn't even mention Broglin Castle, she was determined not to revert to her phone. She felt that the scholars would not approve of Google-aided research.

After several fruitless minutes, Nancy slipped the book into her bag, deciding to follow Saw Wah into the Egyptian display rooms. Two paces into the first chamber, she heard a muffled clicking sound, coming from the furthest display cases. On instinct, Nancy turned and left. She would wait outside on the bench after all.

...

Tom and Sally were waiting for them at the office door. Down a short corridor behind the cubbyhole was the biggest 'lift' (as the English called elevators) Nancy or Saw Wah had ever seen.

It was almost the size of their apartment - padded from floor-to-ceiling, notwithstanding a few tears and stains. "To protect the artefacts. Some of them are quite big", explained Tom.

The chamber descended slowly, loudly creaking. Halting with a slow-motion jolt, the doors opened onto a long wide corridor. Beneath the streets of London, low-wattage lamps illuminated large locked double-doors.

"India, ancient ... India, modern - a relative concept, that ..." Tom indicated the rooms as they walked past. Sally grinned.

They came to the last room on the right. "India, miscellaneous, adjacent and questionable. This should be it."

Tom unlocked a bolt, reached round the corner, flicked a switch and they were standing at the edge of a deep and high-ceilinged room. The lighting here was even less generous, barely extending to the back wall.

A background musty smell. A cornucopia of collectables: dozens of Buddha images - several larger than life-size. Along most of one side of the room, shelf upon shelf of pots and plates. Beyond these, Nancy recognised the shadowy outlines of carved doorframes. Three shelves of small lead opium weights, mostly in the shape of the sacred Brahman duck – the hamsa. She had noticed half-a-dozen of these on display upstairs; here there were hundreds.

Off to the left were three trestle tables joined together. At one end, pots of paintbrushes and more bits of bowl and pottery.

"Restoration work in progress.

But they should have put this away" – Tom takes a small figure from the table, and places it on a nearby shelf.

"Ugly thing really."

Beyond the tables, a row of giant metal filing cabinets, much bigger than those at BurmaAction. These were more like the giant metal boxes she had dusted at the university - but older, with flakes of rust around the handles and hinges.

Tom produced a large bunch of tiny keys.

"Fingers crossed!"

After unlocking the first cabinet, Tom located a couple of table lights, which greatly aided their task. Soon, the four of them had dozens of prints and etchings spread out before over the tables.

"I knew it. I knew it" - Tom was in his element.

"Old Jackson never saw the point in cataloguing these old prints. Fair enough - would have taken half a lifetime's work."

He paused. "Perhaps a quarter. Anyway –"

Tom opened another draw, and carefully lifted out more wide, thin cardboard sheets. Pressed lightly within, sometimes beneath tissue paper, were etchings and some brittle, fading watercolours. Portraits

- presumably, of the long dead. Images of colonial buildings, fringed with palms and other exotica.

"We're in British India!"

Shortly after - "Bingo! - Burma."

A couple of prints showing the great Shwedagon Pagoda in Rangoon, one replete with crouching tigers in the corners; some commercial·posters featuring a native girl puffing giant cheroots, advertising Burmah Oil.

"Are we getting any closer, Nancy?"

She wasn't sure. This had seemed like a good idea - but really, what were they looking for?

"Er-"

And then she saw it –

Ratcliffe Garden - 1828.

Ornamental flowerbeds, ladies and gentlemen perambulating in their finery (such strange hats), a grove of trees, a clearing, and towards the corner – there was the bell, hanging from an unrealistically spindly branch.

"That's it - that's it!"

They crowded around the etching. Tom did a quick check of the items stored nearby.

"Just the one, I think."

They were not allowed to remove it, obviously. But Saw Wah took plenty of photos - although that was not strictly allowed either.

"So - that's what you two were looking for, right?"

"Yes – I suppose so."

Was that it?

'Thank you so much.

Are there any pictures of what was written on the bell?"

They searched a few more sheathes. There didn't seem to be.

"What next?" asked Sally.

She and Tom were obviously waiting for an explanation. Nancy despised a lie, and had almost never told one. She had prepared a short speech about the need to connect with her beautiful and violent, benighted and hopeful homeland - its history. Not untrue exactly, but ...

She hesitated. Saw Wah thought he would have to say something.

Then - "What's this?"

Nancy was looking at the old etching through a magnifying glass provided by Tom - as much as anything, so she could gather her spirit, and her thoughts. She spotted minute letters among the shrubs, offset from the small image of the bell. The curlicues of script were artfully inscribed to look like ornamental vegetation.

"Papun!" - and something else.

"H – a – r ...

Harlan House, I think.

Yes - Papun, Harlan House.

Harlan House, Papun."

Aha – now she knew.

Nancy was beaming as she turned to her husband and new friends.

"I knew it!

I'm sure I went there as a child.

That's when and where I saw the bell.

It's that big, broken-down place on the hill, just on the edge of Papun town, right my dear?"

Saw Wah wasn't sure, but - "Yes ... at least, I think so, yes."

She knew she should elaborate.

"It's just something connected to my childhood. After everything that's happened in Burma ..."

Not much the wiser, Sally and Tom were nevertheless content. The lovely Nancy was satisfied - properly, openly smiling for the first time since either had met her.

They began to put the sheets of card and yellowing paper away, Tom jotting in a notebook.

Momentarily, the lights flickered and went out. A chill spread through the room. Nancy recognised a distinct stink.

A moment later, the dim illumination was restored.

"Not to worry. The wiring down here's pretty ancient - like everything else!"

Not the first time he had told that one either. Sally chuckled obligingly.

Nancy and Saw Wah were pleased to soon depart.

As they returned the Ratcliffe Garden print to its vail of tissue, Saw Wah noticed something written on the back in faded pencil. Sally followed his gaze.

"Seppwood and Sons - 27 Eastleigh Street.

That's just round the corner - unless it's been knocked down."

...

The Count was in his dungeon.

He was intrigued. As with the Princess Tatiana back in old Tartaray (and her delicious husband), he was torn between the desire to torture and destroy one so interesting and beautiful, and the awareness of unnecessary risk. He enjoyed the pang of appetite and trepidation.

There was something about this Nancy.

What was she up to? Did she even know about the treasure?

He must reclaim his horde, stolen by Silk – especially the rubies. Not easy, now that Silk is dead – this time, properly dead.

And this was the girl who had finished him off. His enquiries led to no other conclusion.

Was this child - this Nancy - onto him? Hah - let her try. He would prove a more formidable opponent than Silk.

And good riddance to that thieving busted. Despicable: waiting until the Count's long sleep, before stealing the gold and rubies, stashing them somewhere in bloody Burma – only then turning to his own internment.

Smart though. Having stolen and somewhere stashed the horde, Silk had waited out the 20th century, like the Count. How annoying he had been killed not long after re-awaking - before the Count could seize back his treasure from the thief.

This meant he must return sooner than planned to Burma, to Papun. In the middle of a war zone. Rebel headquarters, or something like that. This could be fun. Necessary, anyway.

Connections overt and covert had been established with the Burmese junta. He knew very well how to tweak the levers of fear and greed - especially fear.

As had Silk.

All his fault. Good riddance - but also one less of their own still going.

Very few of us old ones left, at least above the ground. Most perished centuries ago, in babbling bloodlust idiocy - or worse, by the stake – or worse still, in the fire. But some of us prospered in the darkness.

We had good times in Madras and Pondicherry – the Count and the baronet, Silk. Great feasting. The early days in Burma were a hoot. Pirating around Mergui; juicy blood stakes - playing with the king's enemies in his dungeons. A jolly massacre (mostly of the English), then the French took over in Mergui for a year. Then they in turn were out – but by that time we were back in India.

Ah - the 17th century. Before the dull British consolidated - there was space for a dashing ever-young man in those days.

'Perfidious Albion' – ha! He was master of perfidy.

And always ready to master the new. That was the trick of it – staying up to date.

There was a lot to catch up on this time round. Modern life had much to recommend it. The internet was useful for research, travel and shopping (especially rare books) – and for doing evil. More tedious had been resurrecting his ancient investments (mostly land, gold and precious artefacts) - time-consuming, especially at first. Now mostly the work of Familiars. His precious books.

He remembers the joy of the printing press, first encountered after his first stint in the east. The Count had returned to ancestral affairs - and warfare - in Europe. More fine un-living; secret missions to Kiev on behalf of a king. And books of secret lore.

Back in Burma in the 1800s, he had teamed up again with Silk. At one time they ran some two dozen Familiars. The Raj - and Burma - had treated them well.

But then that bustard ripped me off! Treacherous, dead-dead Sir Robert Silk, Knight of the Great Beast.

And he, the Count, had slept through the whole betrayal.

The Count returned his attention to the young man in chains, hanging before him, one arm torn off and one eye missing. He gave the other eye a good poke.

A weak scream. "When were you born? Mid-1990s?"

Just as well to have missed the 20th century. Not conducive to their Kind. But the 21st was shaping up more amenable. Things were falling apart - floods and fires - desperate starvations - appalling bargains to be picked up cheaply. Intrusions of the state are in abeyance. Easier to live between the cracks. Good times for a vampire in the flush of maturity.

Although most human blood these days tasted just a bit off – plasticy, he had learned was the word. No wonder their sperm count was falling - at this rate, we will be the last ones left.

Anyway - how did this Nancy do it? With iron and righteousness, it seems.

She must know something.

He will be patient and cunning - set his eyes on her, and follow her to the treasure. Then he'll rip her throat out. But not quite yet. He had all the time in the world, with good planning and a bit of luck.

The Count had one or two loose ends to tidy up in England, a year after his longest sleep had ended. The latest victims would be dispatched swiftly. Good sport. The expense was infinitesimal.

Meanwhile, London was flooding again - not good for most vampires. His boss Familiars - Jikes and Jakes - are occupied rehousing the spare coffin, and blackmailing a Duchess.

Last night the Count had kept his spirits up by draining a homeless man in Wandsworth, while fantasising about other victims.

This was more like the real thing.

He licked his lips, and jabbed hard into the weeping, bloodshot eye.

...

27 Eastleigh Street - the printers' long-ago address.

Nancy and Saw Wah stroll past. A solid-looking townhouse. Varnished black front door up steep steps; shuttered ground floor windows. No sign of life. No bell, no answer to their knocks.

They walked back to Bloomsbury through the rush-hour - she to work, he to catch a bus home.

"See you this evening, my darling."

"Yes, Nancy. And be careful."

...

They have been spotted by the bald and flabby-strong Jikes. The Eastleigh Street address was a false lead - but the Count had wondered if clever Nancy would pick up the clue.

A few weeks earlier, wing-ed Sgargov had removed the other two etchings in British Museum storage picturing the bell – leaving just the one, so as to check if anyone was on their trail.

Sgargov's minions were everywhere amid the vaults and crypts of London. That evening the Bat Lord Sgargov feasted on forearms in the basement.

The Count had been sure that Nancy would visit the Eastleigh place, probably with the husband. His Familiar had confirmed it.

Boss Jikes is a retired Metropolitan police officer. He has suckled on the blood, so is shackled to the Count's will. Jikes resents being below a bat in the Count's entourage - but too late to turn back. Unless one believed that stuff about forgiveness and redemption, which Jikes could not.

No further leverage is required, but the Count is in possession of certain photographs which do Mike Jikes no credit. Having escaped by the skin of his teeth last time, the Familiar had no desire to face a paedo-policeman's lot in prison.

"So - get on with it."

Jikes belched loudly - "sorry, sire." He swallowed the rest of a chewy tarantula leg, wiping his mouth with a frayed sleeve.

"Well sire ...

...

In Tattenham, Nancy and Saw Wah are eating pickled plums, and looking up vampires on the internet. Thunder rumbles distantly.

Something blackly flapping catches Nancy's eye - through the window, across the street.

"Nothing that I can see, my dear." Saw Wah pours fresh hot water into their jasmine tea.

Nancy yawns - "Let's get an early night. I have a double shift tomorrow."

Saw Wah is helping friends redecorate an apartment in Kensington. Well paid work Nancy is finishing work with BurmaAction. Things are shifting.

Should Nancy wish, of course they will go. A delayed honeymoon back in Thailand – and across the border into Burma. They aim to make it through the war to Papun.

They have a few thousand pounds in savings, which they were planning to use for a deposit on a flat. Some of it they've given away already. They were never going to find a place cheap enough - not in London, anyway. They will use this money to fly to Thailand, and maybe on to Burma overland. Another donation also for the refugees of course.

To Thailand - the kingdom which had offered them each a kind of shelter for a while, after the terror in Burma.

That night in her dreams - vision of the Green Dragon, and weirdly glowing rubies in the dark.

Part Two – Thailand and Burma

Chapter 3

The Count was enjoying a bubble bath with two ladies of the night, in a private suite just off Soi Cowboy. Trickle of blood on marble - scarlet drops in white foam. Rain drumming on the penthouse panes.

Bangkok was flooded, but he didn't care. He had stashed his Earth and a lightweight travelling coffin in a different, larger penthouse on the edge of the city, not far from the new container port. Then out for the night.

He would play with them for a while, then gorge on Noi and Suzy. The slightly older one had a delicious spirit. There was a sadness about the younger one, Noi - a yearning for not of this world. He would not tell her he was doing her a favour. He knew that wasn't true.

The Count reflected on how disgusting they would look, later - sacks of skin, bristle and bone. Which would have to be disposed of. First though, some fun.

Tonight - his first in Asia for a century-and-a-half - the Count would sleep on ancient silk. Probably the Madras red. He deserved it after the 'red-eye' flight. Irreplaceable, of course - except through theft.

How amusing to have read an article on the aeroplane by that annoying Van Helsing, in some obscure anthropology journal. But the girl is more dangerous, and intriguing.

He had thought of Nancy often in the last thirty-eight hours, heading east always into the night. Some re-routing had been necessary - to fly into Bangkok early evening, and throw any busybody off the scent.

He had manfully (ha ha) refrained from taking a shy young man in a quiet lavatory at Tokyo airport. So the Count was peckish, but not overly so. He had once gone a fortnight without feeding, then devoured a bevy of virgins. These two did not have quite that red-blooded zest -

but were adequate for tonight. He wanted to stay incognito for a while; good to stock up on the red stuff.

...

After dinner the Count read for a while, then brushed up with Thai, Burmese and Karen language apps. Being 504 years old (plus forty years before his un-birth), he knew a lot of languages.

As shortly before dawn each day, he sprinkled a small handful of Earth across his resting place - tonight, the red silk shawl.

In the old days, his Kind had to carry their native Earth in bulky and breakable jars, or trunks for larger consignments. How convenient these synthetic fabrics. The Earth's corruption of any organic substance except the very hardiest of varnished hardwoods partly explained the necessity of coffins. These days, Earth transport was much easier: a modified backpack carried nearly a year's supply halfway round the world.

Although the Count did not plan on being in Thailand - or for that matter, Burma – for that long. He missed the coolly putrid vaults of Europe.

Am I getting old? Keep adapting Cornich.

Soon he would be in the thick of it. To Rangoon in the evening.

The Count was slightly annoyed with himself (he was the only object of his own emotions). He had meant to linger over Suzie, but in the end she had suffered little.

The Count licked his lips. "Remember to have fun, old boy."

...

Seven hundred miles to the north, Chiang Mai had flooded a week ago - the deluge having worked its way downriver to Bangkok. Scores of Shan construction worker families from Burma had their temporary shelters washed away when the Mae Sing River burst its banks on the edge of town. Half-a-dozen slum-dwellers drowned, plus an elderly couple whose house collapsed.

Two weeks of exceedingly heavy rain each afternoon and evening -

after an unusually long, hot summer. There had been none of the usual New Year rains in mid-April, at the height of the dry season when the skies around Chiang Mai rolled with dry thunder. It had stayed hot, dry and smoky until July – when the heavens opened.

Nancy thought she must be getting soft. The sight of a dead dog floating by on floodwater almost made her cry. She had seen worse things.

She had killed a vampire!

Nancy mopped her brow with the end of the turban wrapped around her head.

"You got me doing housework after all!" - smiling to her husband.

"Although it's not my house - as usual!"

Saw Wah was in the other corner of the large room, sodden papers and flood debris littered around, pools of mud across the floor. The walls were already turning to mould in places, although the place was slowly drying up.

Mr and Mrs Wah had not fared badly in the floods, holed-up in their small rented third floor apartment on the edge of town, with rice and dried foods and not too many power cuts. It had been a bit like Covid lock-down.

They were helping out at Humanitarian Relief Direct, their new employer - trying to get the office usable again. Nick from Ipswich had asked any of the staff who could to come in this weekend and clean up, so they could re-open the place on Monday.

Nick continued their earlier conversation, while inspecting power sockets with a screwdriver. Nancy hoped he knew what he was doing.

"But you really should you know - better sooner than later. When you go back to Britain - if you go back.

Saw Wah - you know I'm right."

"You are right, Nick. I'm always telling Nancy that.

She should finish her degree."

"Yes - but you know it's not that simple. I can't just pick up where I left off years ago! In Myanmar!

I would have to start again - in English."

Nancy bore down upon a stubborn knob of grit and dirt.

"I did take a few courses, in England."

Nick straightened from his poking. He looked about to pick his nose with the screwdriver, then thought better of it.

"All of which you passed with flying colours, right?

So - sort out the funding, and go do a de-gree" - he said it like that – "When you get back to England."

"Yes Boss." Nancy mock salutes him.

The prospect was daunting. She had been top of her class before dropping out at the end of her first year at Yangon University. But that was long ago, in another life.

Since then, Nancy had enjoyed taking A-level physics and English, and not done badly. Also the secretarial course had been very useful. Maybe Nick was right - she should be more ambitious. She should have taken a history course as well.

Nick isn't her boss. Although he probably gets paid more than Nancy.

Their boss is Kevin, in the next room - busy on his laptop and phones. In tomorrow morning's staff meeting, Kevin will summarise for them the think-piece he's working on today for *The Irrawaddy* magazine, while the rest of them clean up after the flood.

"Woman's work is never done", sighs Nancy. But she quite enjoys it. She and Saw Wah will go to church this afternoon and cook together tonight.

Tomorrow morning is important. She has a slot in the start-the-week staff meeting to pitch an idea. Saw Wah will come along for moral support. Usually on a Monday, he would be off with the WASH team, visiting ethnic Karen and Hmong villages in the hills outside Chiang Mai, where HARD is working with the locals to install a new WATSAN system.

...

The HARD heads like Nancy's idea - not least, because of the access it promises. Next month Nancy and Saw Wah will travel down to, and discreetly across, the border - to celebrate the 75th anniversary of the Karen revolution, near Karen National Union headquarters at Baw Moo Hta on the Lawtan River, tributary of the great Salween. Nancy will meet one of HARD's local Karen partner organisations. Kevin to accompany them, together with Charlie, the Thai-Karen driver-fixer.

Hopefully, she will get to meet her cousin Philip, for the first time since childhood. Now Lieutenant-Colonel Philip, a rising personage within the KNU, recently appointed to the organization's Central Standing Committee. With any luck, Kevin could meet Philip too.

...

Two months later, waiting in the car for Kevin to finish his cornflakes, Saw Wah asks the other three (in Karen, just in case) – "Couldn't we just speed off, and say we thought he was going to meet us there, after he finishes breakfast?

'An unfortunate miscommunication' [switching to English] - More fun without the kola wah. And you will have to spend all day translating for him, darling."

"Well - he is the boss you know. And I want him to meet Philip."

Nancy wondered what her cousin would make of him.

"Kevin's not too bad. I've worked for worse."

Charlie of all people. But then, he had - much worse. Charlie entertained them on the road with stories of the border (edited for Kevin's sake).

The road twisted south along the Thai side of the river, past Thai-Karen villages and rice fields. At a couple of points, off to the west in Myanmar they saw smoke rising - presumably from a battle beyond the hills in central Karen State; once they caught the distant sound of gunfire. There were several Thai military checkpoints along the way, expertly navigated by Charlie.

Seven hours out from Chiang Mai, they pulled into a dirt lane behind a couple of noodle stores, a few dozen kilometres north along the border from Mae Sot town. Behind the shacks, scores of pickup trucks and hundred motor-scooters and bikes were parked along the riverbank, with people milling around.

...

Hot and sticky, fifteen minutes later they stood in the shade of huge clumps of towering bamboo. A nearby signboard proclaimed –

Welcome to 75th Karen Revolution Day - 31 January 2024

Back in Burma!

It was supposed to be the beginning of the hot dry season. But the weather was changing, with rain most weeks. As they gathered their bags from the riverbank, the first few drops began to hit.

"Not good for the farmers if this keeps up" knows Saw Wah.

When the shower stopped and the sun came out it was steaming hot and humid. They checked to see if their phones still worked. Just about, but only for texts.

While Nancy and Kevin went to find Philip, Saw Wah and Charlie slipped away.

"Message me if you need anything.

Yes, yes - we meet at the Karen Women's Organisation stall at 8 PM, if not before."

Nancy's husband and Charlie had already bumped into a friend of a cousin, with whom they ambled off, arms slung around each other. Beyond them on the other side of the parade ground, before the giant processional bamboo arch, a long row of temporary shops lined the dirt road connecting to KNU 9th Brigade headquarters, around the corner and up the hill. (KNU HQ proper was a little further upriver, in the shadow of some useful cliffs.)

Nancy drank tea with Kevin, waiting for the Lieutenant-Colonel and trying to catch up on the news - hampered by having to translate for the ever-inquisitive kolah wah. A new Federal Democratic Army Headquarters had been established under KNU protection at Papun, which was now the provisional capital of both Kawthoolei and free Burma. Guarded by the KNU, Federal Democracy Alliance leaders were gathering in the town to discuss a new constitution for Burma.

The bulk of anti-coup forces in this part of the country came from, or operated under the command of, the KNU - with some reinforcements from allied groups in the north. Nationwide, dozens of People's Defence Forces battled the junta daily, in addition to the longer established Karen and Karenni, Kachin, Ta'ang, Mon and other ethnic resistance armies. The PDFs were mostly young 'Gen Z' people from the towns and cities – many from the Burman majority community, who had fled after and to fight against the coup. Among them were some of Nancy's old comrades.

Increasingly battle-hardened and better armed, the PDFs had surprised many observers with a string of hit-and-run victories against junta forces. At the same time, the KNU and allied ethnic armed groups had launched further daring attacks, stretching the Myanmar Army further than any time since independence – striking deep into the lowlands, liberating many areas from the enemy. The junta had responded with vicious airstrikes against civilians, as well as insurgents - but morale was nevertheless high.

Some PDF leaders were here at Baw Moo Hta, to show solidarity with the KNU's long struggle for freedom. These included an old friend. /

Ma Bella said that Nancy looked healthier than when they last met.

"You were just skin and bones back then, sister.

Married life in England suits you!"

Nancy shrugged - remembering terror and pain, mortar fire and gunshots.

Back then, on the eve of the 2012 ceasefire, the KNU had been losing territory for years, barely holding on to desperate positions in the jungle - although the resilience of villagers and insurgents was extraordinary. Following the ceasefire, then nine years later, the coup, the KNU was back at war again, and anti-junta forces were resurgent.

In recent weeks the Myanmar Army had clawed back some territory. In Chiang Mai, they had heard about the attack on Myaing Gyi Ngu, which the KNU and allies liberated last year. Fierce fighting was underway street-to-street, as they sipped hot beverages and caught up with the news.

To the north, the Kachin Independence Organisation still held Bhamo – capital of Kachinland. Many lives were lost in heroic defence against a massive Myanmar Army counter-attack, but the KIO - close allies of the KNU - had held on. As in Karen areas, ground-to-air missiles had been a game changer. (It is assumed that China looks the other way.)

Then - here was Philip.

She recognised his smile. Philip wore a blue Karen longyi and plain yellow T-shirt. A bodyguard trailed discreetly behind.

"I was hoping to see you in uniform."

"For that, you will have to wait until tomorrow" - that same sweet smile.

She switched to English, introducing Kevin.

For the next 45 minutes Kevin plied Philip with sometimes clumsy questions, some of which he pretended not to understand. Nancy translated. (Although Philip spoke good English.)

Then Kevin asked if they would like more drinks. "Oh yes please - it's so hot. Another cold Lanta would be lovely.

Philip?"

"Yes please."

They were sitting on plastic chairs in front of the Karen Woman's Organisation stall. This housed a display documenting the military regime's human rights abuses, portraits of leading Karen and other women of Burma and the revolution, and photos of KWO activities. Among several certificates, framed photographs and medals along one wall, the 2022 UN Women of Justice award. Visitors drifted by in small groups.

Instant coffee, Milo, Burmese tea and a selection of pastries and friend snacks were available at the counter. No cold drinks though, so Kevin had to walk back up the row of stalls to find one selling sodas from an ice-box. This was fine with him: Kevin's head was full of Philip's interesting information, some of which he wanted to scribble in his notebook unobserved, before going back for more.

Nancy and Philip talk about the family. They are dispersed, but mostly doing okay all things considered - thank God. Surviving grandparents back in Yangon, keeping a low profile in case the secret police take an interest. Nancy's own father (a widower and retired schoolmaster) sick at home, never having properly recovered from Covid.

Suspecting Kevin's imminent return, Nancy gets to the point - "I ask one thing for me, dear cousin - if I may. This is just for me, nothing to do with Kevin and the NGO."

That smile again.

Nancy sticks to English: chances are that anyone listening won't understand.

"I need to go to Papun - but I can't tell you why. Can you help me?"

A pause, the smile. "Cousin, it doesn't really matter why.

It's just not possible. Too dangerous.

We're expecting a counter-attack any day. Maybe they are going to try and outflank us while we focus on Myaing Gyi Ngu.

That's what the boss thinks, and he's usually right."

Nancy was about to appeal, to reassure. Perhaps Philip thought she was planning to lobby the constitution-drafters in Papun, or get a 'sinsta-scoop'? But here came Kevin, balancing a plate of cakes atop three cans of soda.

"Sorry Nancy.

And watch out for that kola wah. Presumably, you know what they are like."

"I'm married Philip!"

...

Nearly midnight. The Count is at the Siam Society library in Bangkok, reading accounts of the East India Company and renegade English traders along the 17th century Tenasserim seaboard, in the Mergui Archipelago. The Count indulges reverie.

They called us 'interlopers' - we were privateers.

Trading with the King of Ayutthaya; trading with and raiding the British and the Javanese; scheming with and against the French - who burnt the Count's cousin at the stake; out with their tongues, stuffed down their throats while he drained le Capitan. They shipped timber and ceramics, spices and opium, gold and guns, slaves. In treacherous partnership with Sir Roger Silk ... ah - the massacre at Mergui.

His nostrils twitched.

A change in the air. He sniffed deeply.

The Count closed de'Caan's rare edition of Mercellier's *Second Benedict Mission*. Jungle steam and sulphur drifted off the pages.

A young lady in shadows at the far end of the reading room. A late librarian.

An instant later he is inches from her. She pauses, returning a book to the stacks.

For fun he hisses.

Khun Phaen spins round, shoulder-length black hair bobbing - a frightened smile on her pale lips. The Count gives her a moment to appreciate the situation - fangs drawn, eyes glowing molten.

Her head thrown back, her throat exposed. Fangs slash razor-deep into pulsing flesh. Phaen gasps and swoons in delicious agony and terror - he drains her with ravenous passion.

Soon she is crumpled on the floor. Blood over much of his face and some on her clothes.

The Count savours afterglow.

He steps back to survey the corpse.

Another quickie.

This had been fun, and nourishing - but clear-up presented logistical complications, and minor risk. Unprofessional.

Still, they were easier to butcher once drained and crumpled.

The Count jammed a chair temporarily against the door-knob. He took newspapers from the reading racks, spread them under the young woman's body and set to work with the small axe.

Tomorrow night a chartered military flight would take him to Yangon. This evening he had some banking and other arrangements to complete. Time was of the essence.

...

Karen-4-Karen, the local partner organisation, had some floorspace and spare mosquito nets at their office, not far from the parade ground. Nancy was content, sleeping on plastic mats on the floor again after all those years in beds. Cosy inside the mosquito nets.

When the bugle sounded before dawn the next day, Kevin emerged first. "Good job I brought the earplugs!" – removing and displaying little blobs of dirty orange foam.

Saw Wah staggered out from under the netting, and went looking for hot water. He knew that Kevin had brought proper coffee with him

– a taste for which was one of the few vices Saw Wah had picked up in England.

Nancy had a cup of jasmine tea, then off they set for the parade ground. Fortunately, there had been no more rain overnight.

A path led from the bamboo and leaf-thatch office, around a clump of bushes, and onto a wider red dirt road, which passed through the archway –

Welcome to Karen Revolution Day.

By now, they were in a slow-moving stream of people, dust kicked up by a thousand flip-flops. Mostly Karen folks; many - especially the women - wearing traditional tunics and longyis. Maybe a quarter of the men - and a few women - in uniforms.

A handful of kola wah - some looking awkward in Karen costumes, sweating already. A few Thais, mostly identifiable by their clothes. Some were spooks or business-people looking to pick up cross-border trade deals; others were sympathetic locals from across the border or KNU spouses.

After entering through the bamboo archway, Nancy and Kevin did not turn right like most of the others, to find a place along the side of the parade ground - hopefully in the shade. Instead, they peeled off to the left, making their way to the back of the podium. Saw Wah was not inclined to follow.

"Oh come on - this will be fun."

"Maybe for you - but not for me. I'll see you afterwards."

One of Philip's men spotted them, and guided Nancy and Kevin to seats at the back of the podium. Half-a-dozen ranks of chairs separated them from front-of-stage, where dignitaries were preparing to make speeches. On the other side of the parade ground, already half-lost amid the reddish dust and morning haze, thousands were settling in for the main event, jostling gently in the receding shade.

The ageing KNU Chairman's opening speech railed against the junta and their appalling abuses - rallying the Karen and other progressive forces for one last push this dry season. Cheers from the crowd - although Nancy was not sure the under-powered PA system could reach that far with clarity.

Several representatives of fraternal Ethnic Revolutionary Organisations where here, together with a smattering of foreign donors and even some adventurous diplomats. The foreigners did not make speeches.

Plenty of resistance leaders did. It was past 9 o'clock and getting hot.

Finally, public announcements - then a column of smartly-kitted schoolchildren and teachers led the way, followed by a small marching band complete with white gloves and a military brass section. Then rows of tightly-drilled soldiers marched by in fresh fatigues, with new-looking automatic rifles.

Philip appeared at her side.

"1000 fighters from the independent Karenni Republic."

She counted about 600 of the Karenni soldiers (including several dozen women), plus a few officers and bodyguards up here on the podium. The KNU had mustered barely more troops for the parade. But now was not the time to be bringing men back from the front line.

"Now they've won their own freedom, the Karenni have come south to help us.

Tomorrow, they head to Myaing Gyi Ngu."

Nancy saw an opening.

"Myaing Gyi Ngu.

Dear cousin, if I wanted to go there, I could understand you saying no. But from what I hear, Papun is relatively stable.

I don't expect you to take responsibility for me, for my safety - just give me authorisation to go."

This time a frown.

"You've only just got back, Nancy.

Go and help the refugees - the internally displaced people. That's what your NGO friends are here to do, you know."

He tried the smile again.

"Sorry about what I said earlier - about the kolah wah. We don't have so many friends, and most of them are here to help. That Kevin is OK.

You be careful - that's all."

After the parade, Nancy and Kevin slipped away. By early afternoon the HARD team was half-way back to Chiang Mai.

"You know what?"

"Next week I'm driving down to Mae Sot with a couple of the team. Great if you could come, Nancy? But only if you have time, of course."

Excellent: a trip to Mae Sot with Kevin might bring Nancy closer to Papun. Not that she needed the foreigners' permission or help, but this would be good cover.

...

They travelled down to Mae Sot in an old Pajero with an old border hand – a consultant hired to help HARD understand the complexities of this 'protracted conflict'.

Dr Denise Dexter was an adjunct professor at Patton University in Chiang Mai, and author of half-a-dozen books on Burma. She was in full flow –

"These days of course Mae Sot is full of restaurants and bars and the like, and the town has spread way out. There are super-stores and giant car sales-rooms on the outskirts, and new moo baan housing estates. I knew that times had truly changed when they opened the first Starbucks.

A lot of it financed by the cross-border trade. Some Thai military and police types have grown very rich. Maybe some KNU leaders also.

The KNU and a bunch of other armed groups have tax gates all along the border, as you know. And since they've started winning back territory, that brings new opportunities."

Kevin obligingly asked her to elaborate.

"You know, since the 1990s the Thais have heavily favoured the Myanmar Army - but there were always those in the Thai deep state still willing to support the Karen - especially if there's a profit to be made.

These relationships with ethnic minority groups along the border stretch back for ages - centuries, really. What goes around comes around - on a wink and a nod from Uncle Sam. Times are changing. The Chinese are watching warily."

As the world falls apart, thinks Kevin.

"Of course these days Myawaddy - just across from Mae Sot - is one of only two towns along the Myanmar side of the thousand kilometre border still more-or-less controlled by the junta.

The Thais play all sides of course.

It's a shifting and dangerous game. Spooks everywhere."

They talked about how, towards the end of World War Two, some British officers had promised the Karen independence, if they struck against the Japanese.

"Worked pretty well at the time – but the British never followed-through.

Not surprising the Karen took up arms soon after the war - they had the guns and plenty of fighting experience – with zero love lost between Karen leaders and the Burmese nationalists from the lowlands."

Kevin chipped in - "75 years ago! The battle of Insein.

You know we were at the Revolution Day celebrations last week. That's where I met Col. Phillip."

"So you said."

Denise Dexter settled down for a nap - "Could you turn down the music, just a little."

An hour later, pulling into Mae Sot they went over the next day's meeting with KNU leaders. They were there to pitch a new HARD project in Kawthoolei. Kevin is hyped - "Let's do what we can, while we can!"

Around the world, aid money was tightening up as temperatures, sea levels and crises escalated. With London flooding and much of the US burning, Kevin thought there was less than a decade left in the aid business.

"Not many votes left in foreign aid when Western economies are nose-diving. It's only a matter of time until populists in the White House and Downing Street pull the plug."

That said, Myanmar was a partial exception – for now. "The Americans like keeping tabs on China. Useful to have some friends in Burma.

But I don't think the Thais will want the KNU growing too strong."

Dr Dexter got in the last word - "Of course, Thailand has been balancing against China and the US for decades."

...

Saw Wah having stayed in Chiang Mai, Nancy had a room to herself at the downtown hotel. As soon as she was alone she called her contact.

Nancy excused herself from dinner with the team, arranging to meet Kevin and the group in the morning, before heading to the KNU liaison office in a nearby moo baan. And yes, she would try to arrange another meeting with Philip - although he was actually across the border in the conflict zone.

As night fell, Nancy slipped out of the hotel, unconvincingly disguised in a large a floppy hat. The evening was warm – a black bat circling under streetlights.

As instructed, she walked towards the gas station. At exactly 7 o'clock, a battered Toyota pickup slowed down and stopped just in front of her - "Come on, get in."

Twenty minutes later, Nancy sits among a dozen young people in a circle, in the back room of a rented bungalow on the edge of town. A few biscuits, ubiquitous Burmese tea and a few cans of cola.

"You know the donations were non-conditional.

You spend it on what you need most – rice, guns, whatever."

They are speaking in Burmese. Only a couple of Karen here - the rest are from the cities, Burmans and others who fled to join the revolution.

"I know it isn't much – we've been sending money to the KNU as well. But your brothers and sisters in England want me to tell you that we won't give up - not so long as you don't.

We can't do much - but we try our best."

Nancy told the small group about protests in front of the junta's London office (downgraded from embassy status), about fundraising events and social media campaigns. She had already handed over $4000 - latest donation from the Burmese community in London.

"But there is something else I need to ask you - something personal.

From me – for me."

Nancy sensed a change in the room. Thinking the tension caused by her switch of tone, she nevertheless pressed on.

"Look - here's the thing: I really, really need to get to Papun.

Can't tell you why, but ..."

Someone shush-ed her. Already a couple of people were on their feet, heading for the door.

"I'm sorry, but ..."

"Be quiet Nancy."

One of two other women in the room flicked off the lights - but it was too late. As they sat in semi-darkness, car headlights shone full-beam through the flimsy curtains.

Someone was speaking Thai in the next room – quietly at first, then raised voices. A muffled shout, a thump - and the door swung open.

Torchlights and shouting in Thai - a language Nancy didn't understand. The gist of it was clear enough though - the police were here, and they were all under arrest.

...

In the back of the police van, the little group was mostly silent - handcuffed side-by-side on metal benches. Several of them had experienced this kind of thing - or worse - back in Burma.

Nancy thought she knew what several of them were thinking, or at least hoping: whatever happens, we won't die tonight. Better to be picked up by the Thais than the junta's secret police.

According to Ko Naing, whispered - "You and I and Niko should be okay, Nancy. We've got passports and visas. I'm more worried about the others."

Soon afterwards, the van came to a halt - followed by a clang of metal gates. A couple of minutes later they were hauled out into a small compound.

Nancy couldn't make out much beneath the arc-lights.

"You - you come now" - a policeman prodded Nancy in the ribs, maybe with a pen? No – it was a gun.

"I want to stay with the others."

"You – move now - come now!"

Shoved forward from behind, Nancy caught a glance of Ko Naing ashen-faced. She was quick-marched through a side door.

Down a corridor, and into a small room with one high window and no furniture. Another shove, and she was on her own – the metal door locked behind her. Still handcuffed.

Nancy concentrated on her breathing. She prayed for the others, and for dear Saw Wah. She prayed for forgiveness also: so busy these days

- she had not been spending enough time with the Lord. And now look at the mess she was in.

But also - a blessing to have time to thank Jesus and to pray. She sung a hymn softly, in chains on the cold stone floor.

Twenty minutes later the metal door creaked open. The light in the corridor was brighter than the dim bulb in the room. Someone - something - was silhouetted in the doorway. The figure loomed blackly, shimmering.

Nancy felt nauseous. Something tricky with her vision. The glimmering figure collapsed in on itself - a horrible sucking black void – then rebounded, a sickeningly familiar ache in her bones.

For a moment, Nancy's vision crystallised – a tall white man (very pale skin), with thick black hair and a ghastly smile; golden eyes.

A mocking English accent - "Hello Nancy. I've been looking forward to meeting you. You nasty little pig."

The Count sneered, licked his lips.

"I do hope your friends will be all right. So tender, some of them - so disposable."

And then in Burmese, to an unseen other – "Captain - your prisoner."

Nancy rose to her feet, ready to protest this designation. But he – or it - was gone. Replaced by a couple of Burmese in slacks and sport shirts.

Nancy sensed violence, but also an uncertainty in the two new men - a gap.

In Burmese – "Where has the policeman gone? I demand to see the British ambassador."

A smirk from the bigger man.

In English - "You know, we can do anything to you in this room.

A-ny-thing."

Nancy says nothing.

"You need to tell us about your friends, or else this will go very badly for all of you."

The other interrogator, in Burmese - "You have a tourist visa. You are associating with terrorists. If we don't finish you off tonight, that's years in prison."

"Would that be a Thai prison, or one of your stinking holes?

I demand to talk to the British Embassy.

And unlock these" - proffering her tethered wrists.

Nancy was a good deal more frightened than she hoped she was letting on. But also righteously indignant. She thought of dear Saw Wah.

"You are in no position to make demands."

The skinny younger goon spat on the floor.

A whisper from his senior. The change of tack.

"Tell us about the treasure, and we will let you go.

Come on - the treasure!"

"I don't know what you mean."

"If you do not tell us where the treasure is, we can easily lose a couple of your friends next door - starting with their teeth."

"Tell us where it is.

Otherwise I will personally enjoy kicking the shit out of them.

Then your turn."

Nancy knew that they considered her concern a weak point - leverage. They did not understand righteous compassion.

But could they really do that, here on Thai soil?

Nancy knew that if she told them anything, the interrogation would drag on, probably more fearsomely. She would say nothing - for now at least.

The tactic worked. After a few more questions, her interrogators seemed to lose interest. The boss stepped outside for a minute.

Then - "You can go."

"Not without my friends - and I told you: unlock these handcuffs."

To Nancy's surprise, he did.

"This way."

The smaller one led her back out to the compound, where her comrades were filing heads down into the back of the police truck. They had been hooded and badly scared, but otherwise unharmed.

"They didn't even question us."

An hour later she was back at the hotel - minus nearly $500 of her own money, and all the cash her friends were holding, stolen by the cops. (Nancy was cheered to later learn that the money from London was already hidden by the time the police arrived.)

At least they had let everyone go. Nancy said a prayer.

But - who or what had been that thing in the doorway?

...

Much later that night, the Count was at work.

The Mae Sot police had picked up an opposition A-lister. His friends in the junta secret police paid handsomely for the handover from the Thai cops. The Count covered the expense himself.

He may not have got much out of Nancy earlier - but that had been a useful character test. Let's see where she heads next.

Nasty pig. She didn't like that.

Meanwhile, to the matter at hand.

The Count leaned over a slumped and bloody body, strapped to a metal chair. He licked his lips – "Ready for more, old boy?"

...

By the time she got back to Chiang Mai, Nancy had started feeling unwell. Her aching bones reminiscent of malaria, but she had no fever and twice tested negative for the parasite. She is anaemic, and jaundiced - "a sickness of the blood"; her aching leg and head much worse. A jab of phantom shrapnel. Saw Wah wanted Nancy to see a doctor, but she wouldn't.

"This is a sickness of the soul, husband. We must pray."

Kevin sends her to recuperate for a week in Mae Ramon. Some light desk-work for HARD.

A small, mostly Thai-Karen town in the hills south of Mae Hon Sorn, Mae Ramon still has the old Lanna charm – boxy hardwood houses and Shan temples. A few NGO offices, some serving those forcibly displaced in and from Burma. A pretty ornamental lake in the middle of town; some tourist cafes. A busy market, the usual shops, banks and 7-Eleven stores.

Nancy and Saw Wah are renting a wooden bungalow, with a little veranda near a sparkling stream, in a small resort on the edge of town. By mid-week Nancy is feeling much better, but they will stay until the weekend.

Mid-morning, a familiar middle-aged, white-haired gentleman walks in. A glimpse of silver at his breast.

He bows just slightly - "Good morning, Nancy. How very nice to see you again."

Nancy shakes his hand.

"Good morning Dr Van Helsing."

"I hope you didn't mind me getting in touch. Peter Pratt said it would probably be okay."

"Yes, of course."

"As I mentioned in the email, I'm writing a piece about local NGOs and Karen aid groups. I know I don't have to tell you - this is such an important part of what keeps civilians alive in the war-zone.

Some things are best left un-written of course - confidentiality and safety et cetera - but I'm planning a long-form piece for The Guardian. They seem keen, and it's an important but neglected story. Useful for advocacy, I hope. You never know, might generate some funding."

They ordered lime sodas and talked about Burma for ninety minutes, until a sleepy Saw Wah came looking for lunch.

...

The following morning, an email from Prof Pratt. He hoped Nancy didn't mind him putting VH in touch –

He's a decent chap, with hidden depths and much rare knowledge.

The professor was wiring her £700, collected by friends at the university, for the refugees. Sally sent her best wishes. And some incidental news: there been a break-in at the department, with a couple of objects stolen.

Including that lovely figure of Isis you admired. The silly sausages probably didn't know it was a reproduction.

The police had been diligent - but no sign of the stolen objects, which did not have great monetary value.

Second time round they sent a big surly chap, name of Jikes. He asked about you, BTW.

That evening, they had dinner with Van Helsing at his hotel on the Laem River. Nancy was feeling better still, although her head ached a bit.

VH (as he likes to be called) checks a couple of points with Nancy, about the HARD work and some of the local groups they support. He's done a couple of interviews since they last met, which throw up interesting questions and ideas.

And then a change of tack.

"Oh - and I spoke to an elderly Karen gentleman, Saw Joshua. Used to be quite senior with the KNU - involved in the insurgent alliances of yesteryear.

Do you know him?"

She didn't.

"Well, Saw Joshua is getting on a bit these days. But he seems lucid enough.

He told me a great story, about World War Two and hidden gold. Do you know it?

No?

So - when the Japanese army was retreating at the end of the war, some of the stragglers helped themselves at gunpoint to much of Burmese gold, from pagodas and the like - rubies and gems, sapphires et cetera et cetera.

Apparently, at one point there was an English turncoat spy involved. There's a partially redacted dossier in the British Library – India Office, depository V. One of those old-school aristocratic traitors. Apparently he'd been bleeding Burma dry for decades. Timber trade, slaving - all the delights of empire.

Then this Silk character joined forces with the Japanese. A favourite with the Emperor's cousin, apparently."

Nancy gasped.

"Yes - yes, I know, I know - we Dutch had our colonies also."

Nancy blinked.

"Anyway - some of the loot it's said was stashed in secret hide-outs, during the bloody Japanese retreat along the Sittaung Valley, and down through the Bandong and Three Pagodas passes into Thailand, at the end of the war. Hidden in limestone caves and the like.

You can imagine - difficult to transport gold when you're starving and under attack. And how would they get it home anyway? Best to hide it, and come back later if you can. That's apparently what Silk the spy was up to, working hand-in-hand with the enemy.

But it's difficult to dis-entangle fact from legend.

There have been a few bold declarations over the years. A ranking Thai politician back in the '90s claimed to have found piles of gold in the caves above Kanchanaburi, downriver from the Three Pagodas. Not sure what that was about - no one ever showed up any bullion. There was another coup in Thailand not long after.

Some say that hardy Japanese returnees scoured much of the area in the 1950s and '60s. So, any hidden gold is probably long gone now. But the stories persist. Haunted gold, guarded by samurai ghosts. Who could resist such a yarn!

Anyway - Saw Joshua told me about an accident with dynamite a few years ago, resulting in a massive landslide – which kicked off a scramble for newly dislodged gold.

The treasure was stashed in a Japanese train carriage at the end of the war, apparently - and buried right there in a siding, all those years.

This was a bit north of Three Pagodas Pass – along the old 'Death Railway' into Thailand."

VH paused to see if Nancy was paying attention.

She was: why was he telling her this?

"More than half-a-century later, the train was dislodged by the explosion and landslide. You know those KNU guys love dynamite.

This was in the rainy season, says Joshua - ten years back or more. The Myanmar Army hurried to reinforce the garrison - in the middle of the rainy season, before the rebels got wind of the story and tried to liberate the gold.

So says old Joshua."

He pours more wine.

"Enough for me, VH.

We don't drink much, you know - or at least, I don't" - smiling at her husband.

VH continued - "I imagine you have heard stories like that?"

"Kind of - not really ..."

Nancy helped herself to more fried fish and tangy sauce.

Saw Wah understood. He flipped the conversation onto mining activities. Did VH think the KNU should keep digging for gold?

"OK - now they do more small-scale. And they say not using mercury chemicals any more. But still, I think it is bad - bad for the forest, and bad for the people.

But the KNU needs money - to fight the junta. And to feed the people. What do you think Dr VH?"

Like most kolah wah they met out here, VH had views on such subjects.

The topic moved on to London, a city VH knew well. He told a charming story about getting lost in Soho as a young man.

Before they left, his silver-embossed card - "My private and sat-phone numbers."

They split the bill, which Saw Wah thought rather mean.

"I'll let you know if I hear any more about the haunted gold. I might just write something on that.

Anyway - great to meet you both properly. Hope we can do it again."

They had walked out to the hotel car-park. VH seemed on the point of turning to his driver, who was waiting to take the Karen couple back to their bungalow down the road. Really, they could have walked.

Instead, VH stepped into the space between them, and whispered urgently – "Didn't you ever wonder who tidied up after you, Nancy? In Mayfair - after you killed the vampire."

Nancy gasped, again.

"You must have wondered.

My fellow Sykes had been watching Sir Robert for a while. But he was too strong for us. We lost two good men to that monster, the year before."

VH paused, in case Nancy wanted to say anything. She didn't.

"We didn't get many leads from his apartment, I'm afraid. Seems that wasn't the vampire's main lair, and he kept it clean. Some tantalising dead ends.

We missed the chance to wind up his circle - but without the alpha-V, they aren't much of a threat."

He regarded her for a moment.

"However did you manage it, dear girl?

We know the mechanics - more or less - but you have great chutzpah Nancy! You are a pure sprit. To kill such a powerful vampire.

I suppose he thought he could extract information from you, about the work at Broglin Castle.

I assume that you have worked out why."

A further pause.

"Anyway - Silk underestimated you!

Perhaps he was drawn to you. That sometimes happens.

The long-lived ones grow immensely powerful, and darkly brilliant – but they are subject to appalling and compelling passions.

Most vampires are quite immature emotionally, ironically."

VH paused again. Nancy waited.

"There is another thing.

Regarding the Count. He seems to have taken an interest in you."

Nancy shivered.

"I see you know him – or of him. You are right to be fearful.

The Count surely knows that you killed Silk.

But why is he here? Has he followed you all the way from London, I wonder.

Surely not for revenge.

Does he think you have ... something of Silk's?

If so – be very careful my dear."

With that, VH took a half-step back and bowed slightly.

"Good night Nancy – and Saw Wah, good night.

Augustine will take you home.

I'll be in touch, if I may. Call me any time.

Kilda Barry Ben."

"Good night VH - Good night."

Moments later, in the car - "Nancy: what did those words mean - what he said at the end?"

Chapter 4

Nancy and Saw Wah are back in Chiang Mai. She is feeling much better, but still the pains in her head and legs. She often dreams of the jade figurine, and the rubies.

It is Sunday after church. They are having a picnic at the viewpoint below the national park headquarters atop Doi Lui, overlooking the city of Chiang Mai, and beyond to Doi Saket and the hills of northern Thailand. Shimmer of heat and summer smoke, shrieking cicadas.

Saw Wah says Grace for the group - then a potluck of Thai and Karen food. Grilled chicken, sticky rice, som tam spicy mango salad, fresh greens, and dakapaw rice porridge and beef jerky.

Saw Blu Moo is playing guitar, Saw Soe Moo singing. Gospel and country songs, with skits and horseplay in between.

Despite the no-phone rule, a huddle of girls are sitting round theirs' in the shade, giggling as they snap sinsta-pics of the handsome brothers; lots of 'likes'.

Nancy and Saw Wah are sitting under a coconut tree with Pastor Gerald (Thra-doh Ghaey Moo, in Karen) on rush mats. Last week, Nancy came across more clues in the notebook. She is working on the Latin. Fragmentary - still pointing towards Papun, and Harlan House. They have told Pastor Gerald a little, but not all.

Nancy asked if he had ever come face-to-face with true evil. The question fell out of her, too abruptly - but the pastor did not miss a beat.

"Well - that is a serious question, Nancy. Why do you ask?

Consider, dear daughter. Please unburden your heart."

His paused for ages.

"The Lord bless, protect and guide you Nancy.

Dear child - there is only one thing to say about coming face-to-face with evil. You must utterly and completely surrender yourself to the salvation and love of Jesus Christ. Only He can protect you. Trust Him - our Saviour.

Think not of yourself, but trust in God's love for his creation.

Really my dear, it's what we should do every day. Live in Christ, dear Nancy; empty yourself.

You know our Buddhist brethren have one very clever thing: they are supposed to be thinking always on death - its imminence. Of course, they believe in impermanence - while we know we are eternal in His love.

Death, change and love dear child - these are mysteries. Evil is a mystery too."

He took a sip of tea.

"Jesus Christ grants eternal life - through Grace my dear, through Grace.

Build your house on a firm rock, Nancy."

"Thank you so much, Thra-doh."

They sipped tea in silence for a while.

"What may be troubling you, my dear? Is it the old bell in England you told me about? Why is that? I can tell there is more to the story.

You know - whatever it is, you will not be the first Christian soul to face the devil. He is a rotten deceiver, full of stinking lies and foulness.

But you are a servant of Jesus Christ. Stay righteous in his name, and the evil one is powerless."

He blinked benignly.

"Oh thank you, Thra-doh".

His hands on her shoulders - "Lord God bless and protect you, fill you with Grace and righteousness. In the name of our Lord Jesus Christ - Amen."

"Amen."

A moment's silence - "chicken dear?"

Thramu Sae Wah, the pastor's wife.

The char-grilled chicken was delicious, likewise the tea leaf and papaya salad. Nancy was glad to see that no one had brought beer. ("Not on a church picnic, dear husband.")

Saw Wah ambles over, chewing betel nut - a red stain around his lips. "Sorry Nancy - couldn't resist it."

Pastor Gerald mounts a mock frown. Saw Wah grins – and expertly spits a stream of scarlet betel juice through the side of his mouth, into the grass behind them.

In English - "Oh - sorry Pastor. I wasn't thinking. Very rude of me."

Nancy will have words with her husband.

But first, to the ice cream parlour.

...

When they got back to the apartment, an email to Nancy with a document attached.

18th May

Dear Nancy,

It was nice to meet you and Saw Wah in Mae Ramon. I hope that you are feeling better.

I'm writing this from Leh Ler Der village, just outside Papun. There is a KNU base here. They will take me into town this afternoon.

Seems the Karen and Karenni have pushed junta forces back some way south from Papun. But you probably saw in the news that our friends had to withdraw again from Myaing Gyi Ngu, under ground attack and helicopter fire. So for now there is a front-line about halfway between the two towns. Some big clashes a couple of weeks back, with scores killed on both sides. But since then, there's been a lull in the fighting.

You asked me to check whether you can come, and the answer is - yes, but you will have to get here under your own steam. Major Thomas, the 9th Brigade adjutant (Toh Meh is his Karen name) says you would need a pass from KNU HQ, or maybe Brigade headquarters. With that, it's not too difficult to get here at present. That's been my experience anyway. I'm told there's plenty of accommodation in the town, now the convention is finished. Let me know what you decide.

I interviewed some of the villagers who were burnt out after the fighting a couple of weeks back. They are staying in temporary shelters, on the edge of Lah Ler Der and a couple of other villages. The refugees (Internally Displaced Persons) are getting some help from the KNU government and Karen Relief Committee, and from one of the local organisations you introduced me to in Mae Raman. The 'host community' shares what it can.

There are so many needs here. They have teachers and medics, need school-books and medicines. So many stories of terror, suffering and abuse. But the people are wonderful, sharing love and scarce resources. And the KNU do their best to protect the villagers, although of course the war brings suffering on everyone's heads.

I have an article about the IDPs coming out soon in the G. Will send you when it's published.

You may be interested to learn that I interviewed an old Karen lady yesterday, who told a story about gold stolen from Papun at the end of the war. The treasure was disinterred from some secret underground hiding place, apparently. She doesn't know any details, only that someone (or ones) removed a great treasure in the last weeks of the war. She says the gold is cursed, or haunted, and was never seen again. So far, she is the only one I've come across who knows the tale.

Heading into town shortly. Will let you know if I find out more.

Salutations to you and the excellent Saw Wah – VH

...

Back in Chiang Mai for the last evening of their sabbatical. The white marble tiger sits on Nancy's desktop. Saw Wah is at her side.

Rain battering the panes.

"So - we must get to Papun."

She looks again at the photograph of Harlan House from fifteen years ago, the most recent of a small selection available on the internet. From what they could make out, the walls were barely standing, roof caved in and the whole place overgrown.

"It doesn't look much like the picture in the British Museum, does it Nancy?"

"We've followed the clues so far, to here.

Have to see it through."

Saw Wah sighed - "Yes."

He would be more comfortable if he knew what 'it' was.

"But dearest, what about work? And what about your poorly legs? I'm just saying."

"I know – you're right.

It's just - we've come all this way. We have to see it through.

And also - the struggle, the revolution - I want to do more. We should be doing more - not sitting here in Chiang Mai."

Saw Wah was still unsure - although they have already decided.

He kissed her gently on the cheek. "Oh, city girl - you want to live in the jungle, and fight for our homeland!

I was born there, remember.

My brave and beautiful wife, I will follow you anywhere. You know that my darling."

...

Two weeks later, having given short notice at HARD, Nancy and Saw Wah set off at dawn from Mae Raman with two junior KNU officials. They stopped for fried rice on the edge of the small town, and a fortifying slug of whiskey for the boys - then headed into the forest in a four-wheel-drive truck.

They had agreed: don't post - keep it low profile. Although neither of them spent much time on social media these days.

"And no guns – we agreed that also."

"That's right, my dear."

Not for the last time, Saw Wah wished that he had not conceded this point.

They bumped down a muddy, rutted track through streambeds and increasingly thick forest. Nearly at the border.

"You know, I came this way 12 years ago, heading in the opposite direction.

Or at least, I think this was the route. It was dark and I was injured."

They came to the great Salween River.

"Last time I was here was dry season. I remember big sandbanks, like beaches - with bamboo stalls selling all sorts of things along the riverside – down there.

All underwater now - below those rocks and whirlpools, I suppose."

...

An hour later, they were battling upstream against the rushing green-brown river. The 30-foot longtail boat was hewn from a huge log, with rough planks as splashboards. Sticking out the back, a 6-foot 'longtail scorpion' propeller shaft emerged from a massive and incredibly noisy diesel engine.

This was a dangerous season to be boating, with huge rocks and boulders semi-submerged - whirlpools and the risk of wreckage. Last year, a friend of the boatman's had been crushed and drowned not far from here.

They slow down a couple of times to signal KNU checkpoints on the east bank - barely visible through jungle foliage and grey skies, except for the red, white and blue sun-burst Karen national flag. Torchlight flashback signals from the Karen army.

The rain had re-started, so they were grateful for waterproof jackets and strap-down hats. Still, it was cold and they were wet by the time they reached Greah Hta.

Scores of big blue diesel barrels on the sandy riverbank. Some larger buildings on the upper banks, poking through the rain-hazed foliage – a KNU training college and some wooden houses, maybe officers' residences. A red dirt road snaking past these into the forest beyond, a row of bamboo and thatch storage sheds.

The boatman cut his engine as they pulled into the little bay, where some twenty boats were moored or pulled up, paint peeling off splashboards. Several flew KNU flags.

In the corner of the cove a couple of decayed vessels were submerged and slowly rotting beneath the scummy surface. Nancy almost toppled into the shallows as she crossed a makeshift bamboo bridge to reach the shore. Her legs ached after sitting on a wooden board in the bottom of the boat, and before that the long car ride. Good job she had used her lifejacket as a cushion.

They trudged up the dirt road, winding past noodle stalls and little shops selling instant coffee, replacement propellers, nylon fishing nets, beer (discreetly). As the rain came down harder, Saw Wah returned to the riverbank, to ensure their bags were in hand. Nancy found somewhere dry to sit - the hardwood balcony of one of the bigger stores. Rain drumming on the tin roof.

When her husband returned, she was playing with a chained

maquette, tethered in a nearby tree. If she reached to her full extent, Nancy could feed the monkey biscuits through slats in the veranda railings.

"Steady on, Thramu – we'll need those for the journey."

Nancy and Saw Wah had been joined by Captain Reh Doh, who would accompany them to Papun. They drank tepid tea and the captain smoked long, green cheroots on the hardwood balcony, while his men fixed chains onto the four-wheel-drive truck's back wheels. It was going to be a tough slog up the hill with all that rain.

The usual Kawthoolei hurry up and wait, hurry up and wait. But snug for now at least, with rain pattering.

Once last-minute cheroots had been lit, and betel nut loaded into cheeks, they helped a couple of elderly villagers up onto the flatbed. "We'll drop them at the top of the hill, to continue their journey inland on foot."

"Yes Captain - sounds good."

There was some ambiguity regarding authority. The Captain was definitely in charge, but Nancy's travel authorisation had been issued 'priority' by cousin (now Colonel) Philip.

Then they were off, slowly in a cloud of diesel smoke. The three-litre truck belched, and stalled more than once on the way up the hill - which could have been disastrous. It seemed at one point they would need to use the big winch, to get out of a huge 'puddle.'

"Full of snakes in there, I shouldn't doubt" - grinned Capt. Reh Doh, winding up the front window while his soldiers heaved in the sludge. Then they were off again – spraying mud and smoke.

Revolutionary Karen pop music blared out. Saw Wah enjoyed a nap. Capt. Reh Doh checked his fine black hair in the sun-visor mirror, then his phone again, before the signal gave out halfway up the hillside.

"Switching to sat-phone. Safer anyway - it's scrambled." In English – "Encrypted."

Eventually they made it to the hilltop ridge-track, then south on a relatively flat and well-maintained dirt road along the watershed, through a handful of small Karen villages nestled amid terraced rice fields. Forest stretched off into the clouds to their right (west). A KNU checkpoint every few kilometres – bamboo and barbed wire pole across the track; fox-holes.

Two hours later, they reached the 9th Brigade rear base. Their mud-spattered truck pulled up next to a concrete gate-house and camouflaged sentry box. A dozen battered four-wheel-drive vehicles were parked up here, two of them with large machine guns in the flatbed, and a couple of off-road motorbikes.

"Something's up - stay in the car."

Capt. Reh Doh jumped down and strode towards the checkpoint, and beyond to clumps of milling soldiers. As he approached the group, a couple in full-camo jungle kit turned towards him, momentarily reaching for safety catches.

He spoke briefly to a figure in the middle-distance, then returned to the car. They continued past the checkpoint, passing some two hundred KNU soldiers, mostly sitting or dozing on the grass; a dozen laden ponies and two elephants bedecked in RPG grenades.

A gaggle of village porters were squatting in the shade nearby, stocking up on KNU rice and chicken before the long walk. A few of them were gently teasing a couple of bashful young soldiers from a nearby village. (Both of whom were dead within the year.)

The column was heading west, to stay for as long as the rains lasted in the half-flooded Sittaung River valley. With luck and Grace, the KNU would hold the entire Dawna Range and most of the Kyauk Kyi-Shwegyin plane this rainy season - for first time in nearly five decades.

Capt. Reh Doh is confident - "Even if the enemy pilots were prepared to brave our missiles - they would never fly in this weather." Nancy hopes he's right. They will be here for a week.

There was a lovely little hardwood church, the best-constructed building in the nearby village. They were looking forward to evening services. Starting tomorrow, Nancy will deliver a short course on human rights to junior KNU officers, while Saw Wah teaches English in the local KNU high school.

The villagers cultivated pigs and chickens and orchard-gardens. Further inland and to the north, the hill-people were still largely self-sufficient in rice. According to the Captain, "so long as our farmers don't have to flee, Kawthoolei will have food enough."

Nancy was glad that HARD could play a small role here, supporting peer-to-peer learning on new seed varieties and cultivation methods. These would be essential, if the Karen hills were to survive the deepening impacts of climate change. The rains were ever more irregular and intense, temperatures rising. Food shortages were reported across the lowlands.

...

Saw Wah and Nancy on honeymoon at last. Strolls at dusk, hand-in-hand along lush local paths. Wild flowering orchids, monkey shrieks echoing in the forest.

Then back onto the hilltop trail in muddy trucks at dawn, wedged against assault rifles in the stuffy back-cabin. For Nancy, this was supposedly better than standing on the flatbed with her husband - hardly the place for a professional woman.

Up and along the ridgeline with its old-growth trees, then a dirt road down to the Papun plain. The villages here to the south were larger, with orchards and betel-nut groves. Many of the houses are made of bamboo poles and thatch, the previous hardwood versions having been burnt down by the Myanmar Army - often more than once. Some families - in receipt of remittances from the quarter-million Karen refugees in America and elsewhere - have rebuilt in brick and ugly concrete.

In larger villages, the occasional colonial-era building - many churches, hilltop monasteries glowing in the late afternoon sun.

At twilight they pulled into a KNU compound on the edge of Papun town. Packed dirt square with a flagpole in the middle (Karen national flag just lowered, at dusk). Puddles and a few stray dogs - surrounded by a double line of barbed wire and bamboo-spiked fencing. A couple of longhouse garrison buildings to the side, a hefty-looking ammo store half-hidden at the back. Communications buildings back there also, and a lock-up currently housing one local murderer.

Capt. Reh Doh has a house/office here. He entertains them on his veranda, while his wife serves le-peq thouq tea-leaf salad. The Captain will accompany them into Papun town in the morning. After visiting the brigade office downtown, they will head to the pagoda, then onto the ruined mansion.

That evening, Nancy overheard him joking with the lads about the tourist he was babysitting. "But she is Col. Philip's cousin - so best behaviour. No teasing.

And her husband is from round here. You treat them with respect."

...

Early next morning they were joined by a new companion. Naw Bleh was a niece of Charlie the driver. She had recently finished junior college in Thailand, having previously been educated in Kawthoolei and the refugee camps along the border. Naw Bleh was on her way back 'inside', to see her parents for the first time in several years. After that, she would work for the KNU - maybe - as a teacher.

Naw Bleh would travel part of the way with Nancy and Saw Wah, for company and fellowship. After all, the little party had KNU clearance and security.

"Would you like some rice, and this very good chicken-pumpkin curry, before we head into town?" asked Nancy.

"Oh yes please, auntie."

In order to catch up with them, Naw Bleh had been on the road since well before dawn, and hadn't eaten yet. She helped herself to breakfast, while Nancy and Saw Wah told her something of their plans.

They didn't see much of Papun, but still the little group were still late to the Maha Kya-seiq Pagoda. Before dawn a Myanmar Army patrol was reported heading into the hills only twenty miles to the southwest, albeit beyond the KNU-held Ler Plaw mountain.

Not long afterwards, the KNU 908 Battalion outpost at Deh Wah Hta reported clashes; the day before, the enemy had partially burnt down a nearby hill-side village. Internally displaced people were fleeing up into the wooded hills, where KNU soldiers were dug-in with machine-guns, mortars, and landmines.

"Oh no - that's terrible!"

Capt. Reh Doh gave Nancy the look he kept for naive civilians –

"Yes – but the villagers know where the landmines are. They planted half of them!

We rely on landmines to keep the enemy out.

Yes - I know it's against International Humanitarian Law. But this is a real war."

They spent most of day waiting at a tea shop opposite the KNU office. Saw Wah found a pleasant spot to sleep.

By late afternoon, there had been no further reports. Where had the enemy column got to? Philip - just promoted to full colonel, and apparently in Papun - had sent reinforcements up to the lightly-patrolled Cats-eye Pass, just in case.

Something in code on KNU coms. Nancy heard a blessing and "Ahmen" pass between the Karen soldiers. She thanked the Lord for His Grace in all things. Saw Wah whispered - "Hear our prayer, strengthen our hearts, oh Lord."

They knew that many of the villages up here were followers of the old beliefs. That was fine with Nancy - "After all, it's the ancestors' way – that is Karen culture."

Saw Wah thought she was right. Naw Bleh agreed - "Most people in my village are maw-lu paw-la - traditional beliefs.

We Christians get on with them just fine, most of the time. I even have Buddhist friends."

Many of the Buddhists in Papun were Burmans - although plenty of Karen also followed the Lord Buddha. That was fine with Nancy and Saw Wah too. But religion could be awfully divisive, so she tended to steer away from the subject in conversation with non-Baptists.

Nancy could tell that people they met along the way thought it strange that she wanted to visit the pagoda. Research for her future historical studies seemed a thin explanation. She felt more comfortable stating the pagoda as their destination, rather than the nearby ruins of empire. Anyway, this was the cover story she had agreed with Philip.

But why had he changed his mind, and agreed to - indeed, greatly assisted - her mission? It didn't seem like Phillip to stretch the rules for a relative.

...

They arrived at Maha Kya-seiq Pagoda, on a small hilltop at the edge of town, an hour or so before sunset. The golden stupa glinted above a white marble platform. Shallow puddles shone in the low sun, the rain having stopped an hour before. Side pavilions with Buddha figures and images of revered monks. Other shrines with offerings of flowers, fruit and cola to the pre-Buddhist Nats - supernatural but not transcendent spirits. A hushed air of focused peace and sati - generations of prayerful meditation sunk into the sacred stone.

Nancy and Saw Wah set off to explore. Naw Bleh preferred the company of her phone, back in the car with Capt. Reh Doh and his chaps. The captain wondered whether he shouldn't have accompanied them, but already Nancy and Saw Wah were out of sight.

They walked bare-foot (carrying their shoes), clockwise around the pagoda. At each of the four quadrants, steps down to an outer platform - the handrail a Naga's long and scaly-green body, rendered in millions of tiny glazed tiles. The Naga serpent-dragon rears at the top of the stairs, its seven heads protecting the Buddha from distraction at the moment of Enlightenment.

They headed down the south Naga steps. Past smaller pagodas containing the ashes of saintly monks, many toppled and crumbling. There is another platform here, then a semi-plastered archway out of the monastic grounds, and onto a patch of overgrown grass. A narrow track disappears among litter-strewn shrubs and small trees.

Saw Wah leads the way, occasionally using his machete to clear the path, avoiding broken bottles.

"Watch out Nancy.

According to the Captain, it shouldn't be far."

The path winds past piles of crumbling weed-strewn bricks, then opens out onto what was once a lawn - now overgrown with shrubs, brambles and small trees.

Beyond - the barely standing, roofless walls of Harlan House. Illegible graffiti - vines and creepers - generations of rotten leaves and litter.

The doorless double-doorway gapes.

"It looks so stinky."

"Things don't *look* stinky, Nancy.

You wait here."

Her husband strode towards the wrecked house. He gingerly mounted two slimy stone steps into the dark interior, and was out of sight among the shadows.

If ever a place was haunted, this is it. Nancy said a short prayer, then ate the remaining biscuits bought at Greah Hta.

Where had her husband got to?

"Darling – over here."

Saw Wah must have exited the building at the back.

"Come and have a look."

She approached and followed him round the corner of the decrepit mansion, through an opening in the bricks revealed by freshly hacked vines, into a small courtyard. A large dark gap to her right presumably opened into the house – what was left of it.

It was dank in there and quiet.

Saw Wah took Nancy's hand.

"Up there."

They looked up, together – "The bell!"

Swinging from a rust-encrusted socket, much covered in green-grey lichen and severed vines, a bell just like the one at Ratcliffe Gardens. Next to it, a similar sprocket with more vines, but no bell.

As her husband hacked away, distant memories flashed.

How had Nancy forgotten the once-magnificent pile of Harlan House? She was so little when she came here before. In those days, this had been a government-controlled area. Maybe they had walked up the hill in order to enjoy the view. Perhaps they hadn't even visited the pagoda?

She knew this was the Ratcliffe bell's twin - suspended high above little Nancy when she visited a quarter-century ago. The same bell she had tracked through Silk's notebook.

"The Burmese bell!

Another Burmese bell. "

"Looks like it."

A bullfrog growls and leaps from nearby ferns. A few raindrops patter the foliage. Dusk is here.

Nancy is trying to figure it out.

"Maybe they stole the bells when they built the house? And later sent the other one back to England?"

"I suppose that could be it."

"So – 'Beneath the Burmese bell'.

"What do you think, husband?"

Beneath the bell are large grey flag-stones, tufts of moss and grass growing in the narrow fissures between them; small rivulets of rain-water. No signs of disturbance - but then, it had been decades.

The bell was well-hidden here, but who knew how long ago.

"I think ..."

- an almighty crash, followed by heavy machine-gun fire, not far off.

Squawking birds.

An eerie quiet.

"I think we'd better go!"

"What the heck was that?"

"Don't know darling.

Quick: I'll take some photos."

Saw Wah got snapping. More gunfire in the distance.

"Come on - let's go."

They ducked back out of the courtyard, sprinted across the lawn and were nearly at the southern gate when Capt. Reh Doh emerged, panting.

"Surprise attack!

Are you two okay?

Quick! Have to get out of here."

A sharp whistling sound - a ground-shaking explosion - debris and dust beyond the temple's outer walls.

"Come on you two! Quickly!"

They tried to walk at a respectable pace, returning barefoot through the undamaged, still deeply peaceful monastic compound.

...

They drove fast for an hour, up steep rutted back-tracks north of Papun. Nancy and Saw Wah bouncing around in the back-cabin with Naw Bleh, the Captain in the passenger seat working his shortwave radio and sat-phone. Two bodyguards in the flatbed at the back, armed with M-16s and grenades.

At the top of the ridge was an intersection and a checkpoint. A small detachment of KNU soldiers was cooking dinner in the twilight - broken rice (as always), fish paste (fermented, fried with chili), tinned sardines (when possible) and fresh vegetables (mostly from the nearby jungle). Nancy contributed instant noodles and eggs from Papun. The captain handed out cheroots.

The platoon had set an extra guard. No one seemed to know what the recent attack was about. The Sergeant in charge at the checkpoint summed up the general sentiment - "Bloody enemy being bloody enemy."

They left the truck near the dugout under camouflage netting, and started walking. It was fully dark by now.

Capt. Reh Doh's orders were to get them up into the hills, then off the track. The Captain regarded Nancy and Saw Wahs' city flip-flops with disdain. "Don't worry, we'll stop for the night at the next village - only 20 or 30 minutes." Naw Bleh at least had decent walking shoes.

An hour later they reached the hamlet of Dwey Kee. Capt. Reh Doh had sent a bodyguard ahead to find the headman, or whoever had the biggest house.

"Tell them we need dinner. They should kill a chicken. These two will pay for it."

"Of course.

But Captain - what's the news?"

Nancy couldn't shake the feeling that they were being followed.

"Well – still not sure, to be honest.

My orders are to keep you two safe tonight, then back to town in the morning.

You too, Mss Bleh."

Naw Bleh pulled a defiant face - "Blast them!"

The Captain again. "Thramu Nancy - you know that your cousin is concerned for your safety. He said you have to stay out of Papun until this thing has quietened down, which hopefully means tomorrow.

For tonight, we'll stay put."

He lit a cheroot. "But why on earth attack there? Beats me."

They were sitting in a circle on the floor of the village teacher's house. His wife nestled baby and a toddler in the back room, while tending the hearth and chopping garlic with a cleaver. Thra Eh Paw, the teacher, had gone to find a chicken.

"And maybe a little jug of tee dta pwee", suggested Capt. Reh Doh. "What do you think, Saw Wah?"

"Oh yes captain."

He glanced at Nancy.

"And I expect my wife will drink a little too, for her health."

Later, she would have words with her husband. This was not a good example for Naw Bleh. Nancy might be only a few years older, but that meant she should protect and guide the youngster. Still though, a tipple of rice whiskey wouldn't hurt.

"Excellent, excellent" - the Captain clapped his hands.

He re-lit the cheroot.

"Well - it was a surprise attack.

I can tell you that much."

He was enjoying himself.

"Your cousin - Col Philip - is a fine officer and deserves the promotions. But this time he got lucky, I reckon. No disrespect.

KNU coms says 9th Brigade repulsed an enemy sneak-attack. And Col. Phillip did do that - or rather, he sent Lt. Bonnie and the lads up there to hold the ridge, a couple of weeks back, and then he sent in reinforcements double-quick.

But - I'm not sure they were really expecting an attack. Sounds like Bonny was as surprised as anyone.

A couple of our lads were badly injured. Mortar shrapnel."

"Captain - we must pray for them. And for all the brave soldiers."

"Quite right Nancy." And they did.

Afterwards - "So, Captain - what do you think they were up to?"

Capt. Reh Doh started on a new cheroot.

"Were they testing our defences, probing for weak spots? Not the sort of thing the Myanmar Army usually bothers with.

I don't know. Maybe just to keep us busy?

Thank the Lord – and Saw Bonny. His chaps must have put up a good fight, because the enemy pulled back into the jungle after the first clash.

Good job Philip sent them up there. Can't deny that.

Bad news is we don't know where they went, or even how many of them. Enemy didn't stick around.

But in that case, why attack in the first place?

That's no easy assault. It's a tough hack over the Ler Plaw range. Why come all that way, only to retreat?

That's why HQ are concerned. They want me to keep you up here for a bit longer.

Could be worse - eh?"

He and Saw Wah sipped rice whiskey, Nancy jasmine tea.

"And another thing – Saw Bonny says there was at least one kola wah with them.

He didn't see the white man, but a couple of his guys did. Big chap. Not the first time, as you know. Russian, probably. The enemy do sometimes use them in the front-line, but generally they hang back a bit from the action. Good snipers – blast them."

After one more round of htee dta pwee, they ate with Thra Eh Paw. He had news.

A dozen displaced families had just arrived at the other end of the village. They would stay with relatives or in temporary shelters out in the rice fields.

After dinner, Nancy and Saw Wah and Naw Bleh went to talk with the IDPs. The Myanmar Army had burnt down part of their village, a few days before. Luckily, everyone got out alive this time. When the village was last attacked, nearly three years ago, two women had been killed - shot in the back trying to flee.

Then, the enemy had stayed for a week before withdrawing; they stole everything. This time, according to KNU intelligence, the Myanmar Army column had already moved on quickly - so the people would probably start going home tomorrow. Unless the enemy had laid landmines. The KNU would send in sappers first, to check.

"That's not an easy duty", said the Captain.

In the meantime, families from the two villages shared rice and fish paste (provided by the KNU), fresh local greens and chilis. Nancy and

Saw Wah bought instant noodles and super-sweet cookies for the children, from the village store. They played guitar, sang and worshiped the Lord together.

Afterwards Nancy noted to her husband that the animists looked a bit uncomfortable, standing at the back.

"Yes - but they ate the cookies, and I think they enjoyed the singing - even if they don't know the words."

Next time, they would bring schoolbooks, sandals and multivitamins for the kids. Hopefully, HARD could help with that.

Nancy and Saw Wah were tucked-up inside one of the village's few mosquito nets before 9 PM.

...

Up at dawn the next day for toasted rice-cakes and coffee.

The Captain had been awake for some time. Squatting round the clay-brick hearth with plastic cups of instant coffee, he told them the news. There had been another coup in Myanmar.

Three-and-a-half years ago, junta supremo Dim Aung Hlaing had seized power. Last year - after destroying the lives of millions - he was overthrown.

"An internal coup. Shot in the back of the neck by one of his own colonels - headless corpse dumped in the Yangon River.

Some say the fellow did that is a hero."

Then there had been General San Saing - until last night.

"Seems he's out now – replaced by yet another general: Win Tun. Can't say I've heard of him.

The new lot are calling themselves the Council for Restoration of Administrative Procedures. Stupid name.

Apparently, the navy chief and a couple of others have been arrested. San Saing has disappeared – maybe he's dead.

God rot them all."

The thinking at headquarters now was that the attacking Myanmar Army column had probably withdrawn because of the coup. Who knows what moves the new junta would make. Most likely, enemy field commanders wanted to be back at base, to stay on top of the situation and ensure their comrades didn't stab them in the back.

Nancy and Saw Wah would have to stay in Dwey Kee a while longer, while the Captain checked with brigade headquarters what to do. He wasn't taking any chances with the Colonel's cousin. And anyway, it was nice up here.

Last night over whiskey, he had been proclaiming the bounty of Kawthoolei's forests. Along the Thailand border, much of the big timber had been taken out in previous decades. These days, the KNU was encouraging forest regeneration - but it would be a while before they knew if re-wilding would work. Up here though, inland from the river in the high Dawna hills, they were further from trade routes and logging roads. There was still some pristine forest left - even a few tigers and wild elephants. "The real Kawthoolei" - the Captain and Saw Wah agreed.

"Captain - if we can't go back quite yet, couldn't we make a little side trip. I'd love to see the beautiful places you talked about last night.

'Nestled beneath the limestone cliffs', you said. Sounds wonderful."

Naw Bleh agreed with Nancy - "Oh please, uncle - let us go."

...

Later that morning, a call from Philip. A foreign journalist had gone missing - last spotted in the uplands beyond Moo Kee village. A Dutchman - apparently known to Nancy.

"Actually, I've been trying to re-locate him for a while," says Philip.

As the security situation had seemingly stabilised for now, Nancy could make herself useful, and track him down.

"He's sick apparently - this VH.

Assess the situation, report to me - get him back to Thailand."

Now Nancy realised why Philip had changed his mind about her coming.

"And how would I do that - track him down?"

"The Captain will handle that. Your job is to make sure Van Helsing complies."

Philip suggested checking her email for messages, using KNU Sky-com.

"Maybe he's tried to contact you? When I last spoke to him - a couple of weeks ago - VH said you were in touch."

A pause - "You do know him, right?"

"Yes."

Another pause - "Why else would I authorise your trip?

Come on Nancy - keep up."

Philip instructed Capt. Reh Doh to allow her use of his sat-phone.

"Must be important. I've never known him let a civilian do that before."

There was an email from VH.

20 May – 20th ? – Moo Kee

Oh Nancy - I have seen him! In Papun, two days ago –

... only now can I write.

Out of the corner of my eye - the corner of my eye. In the bustle of the market - walking in the light of day.

It saw me - looming shadow stink of abomination. Appalling.

... I think I must have passed out think I must have – again - I heard a million wings ...

... clitter clitter with their claws ...

Don't know how I got back here - all day in bed ...

Nurse says I must rest.

But must get back to Thailand.

Sending this I can send this.

clitter clitter – clitter clatter ...

Dear Nancy.

Kilda Barry Ben

"The poor man is raving."

"Yes, and yet dear husband - we know the threat is real.

We must go to him."

Philip authorised travel to Moo Kee - then straight back to Papun.

Another message that afternoon: VH was indeed sick in Moo Kee village. He had refused to evacuate - but Philip knew that Nancy would persuade him. She was not to worry. The area was quiet, and there was a KNU militia outpost not far from the village, which could be called upon if necessary. A handful of the militiamen lived in Moo Kee.

"Delicious chickens up there, Cousin. Get them to cook one for you."

They set off at once. Along the way, Naw Bleh picked jungle greens for dinner.

The little group arrived in Moo Kee just after dark - faint smell of resin in the breeze, here above the pine-line. Two dozen houses perched on the ridgeline, overlooking rice terraces and orchards, and beyond that the swidden fields and woods. Half have small solar panels; the rest use candles or paraffin lamps. The small church has a generator nearby, but this is only used for religious and other special occasions, and for cramming before exams in the next-door village school.

Naw Sae Ler - the village health-worker and midwife, whose husband is a KNU Sargent - took them straight to see the ailing foreigner.

She didn't know what to make of him - "He staggered into the village two days ago, raving about I don't know what. Something about gold, and ghosts.

Since then he's been mostly delirious, or sleeping. Can't get him out of bed, let alone out of Moo Kee.

He's spent a bit of time on his computer though. He keeps that safely in his backpack. He's got some kind of thingy to connect it to the internet."

His clothes were torn, and it looked like he hadn't eaten in a while – although Naw Sae Ler swore she'd been feeding him rice and chicken soup in small portions.

"I think he might be dying" she whispers loudly.

VH's sunken face was grey, his breath rasping.

After several gentle, then not so gentle nudges, he half awoke. They helped him sit up.

Squinting in the bamboo-slatted half-light, VH shivered, with a blanket round his shoulders.

"Is he dying?"

"Oh no, husband - he will be all right."

Then louder - "You will be all right VH - won't you?"

He turned slowly towards her.

"N-Nancy, is that you?"

...

Not so much that VH refused to leave, but that he couldn't. Naw Sae Ler, who had raised five children and seen two die, didn't think he would make it even to Dwey Kee slung in a hammock - let alone down the bumpy track to Papun.

"And then what?

I don't know what's wrong with him. Dr Kweh Htoo in Papun might be able to help."

That evening VH seemed a little stronger, and swallowed some rice soup. But as the night chill descended, he began to shiver and rave - about gold in the hills, and terror in the darkness.

"Calm down VH."

Nancy helped him to sit up.

"Nancy - you came for me!"

She ran a damp cloth over his brow.

"Shhh - no need to talk. Everything is going to be okay."

"But I must ... tell you ..."

A rattling breath.

"Safe your strength, VH.

Tell us when you're ready."

Nancy said a prayer.

VH seemed to gain a little strength. He smoothed his silver hair with an unsteady hand, composed himself.

"Oh Nancy.

Nancy - it's there. Under the landslide, in the cave.

The vampires' treasure - I have seen it. Beneath the cliffs – in the mud beneath the cliffs."

VH dragged a ragged breath.

"The landslide ... Beneath the cliff Nancy.

That's where you'll find it."

VH slumped back, his lips and fingers trembling.

"He's passed out.

Nancy – he's fainted!"

Naw Bleh checked his weak pulse. VH stirred a little.

"It's okay, sir - it's okay.

Mss Nancy says you are going to be okay."

They prayed again, and sang a gentle hymn. VH drifted into twitching sleep.

...

In the dry season, with a clear path, the trek would have taken only two or three hours. In this humidity, with intermittent rain making its way through the foliage, the going was heavy. Swarms of mosquitos competed for their blood with horrible leeches. After taking a false turn, it was past 3pm when they made it to the limestone cliffs. Then another hour scrambling up muddy hillside tracks before they reached 'the big ear' (as the locals called it).

After consulting with Naw Sae Ler and the village elders, they thought they knew the place. A couple of village lads accompanied Nancy and Saw Wah, Capt. Reh Doh and the two young soldiers.

Last night Nancy had persuaded Philip that the easiest way to assuage VH's ravings, and ease his evacuation, was to do what he wanted and investigate the supposed gold. The Colonel and Capt. Reh Doh were both of the opinion that this was nonsense - but the village elders pointed out there had been landslides recently near the caves, beneath the big limestone ear.

None of the locals had been up there since - not after VH emerged from the forest, covered in leeches, raving about ghosts. They had been planning to - but not yet.

In that case, decided the Colonel, they should set out in the morning. He reminded Nancy that she inspired confidence, and them all that the captain had guns and the authority of Kawthoolei. Capt. Reh Doh had once escaped a Burmese prison, killing two guards with a rusty blade. He was a match for any ghost!

After Philip's little homily by radio, they had another round of tea and/or whiskey on the village head-man's veranda, before bed.

"A Deh Breh lives up there, you know" - the old man slowly refilled his tobacco pipe.

"An ancient spirit.

My father saw him once or twice - but that was long ago.

Maybe he's gone back into the hills. The old ones are retreating these days.

But that is the De Breh's home - or used to be."

The Captain had scoffed, but several of the villagers nodded.

Last night, Nancy dreamt of the De Breh - a luminous presence. And of the sickening rubies.

"Superstitious nonsense", according to Capt. Reh Doh.

"A pure spirit of the forest", said Saw Wah.

Now, pistol drawn, Capt. Reh Do led the way - Saw Wah close behind. Despite her husband's imploring, Nancy had insisted that they leave the guns to the soldiers.

Scrambling up a slew of rock, mud and semi-submerged roots, they cut through tangled rattan, emerging into what they hoped was the right clearing, at the foot of the cliffs.

Drenched in sweat and jungle gunk, Saw Wah cut through vines, brushing ants and leaves off the back of his neck - "Around here do you think, Captain?"

"You are asking me?

If you are asking me, this is a waste of time."

"Have faith, Captain - have faith."

"Faith I have - but this is something different.

And where is your Deh Breh?"

In the past half-hour the sky had darkened. Rain was on the way. Rumble of thunder in the distance.

Capt. Reh Doh took a swig from his flask and handed it to Saw Wah. He was about to give this nice young man a short lecture on the foolish hunches of women and madmen. But just then, off to the right –

"Here! Over here!"

Nancy and Naw Bleh had branched-off ten minutes earlier. Picking her way through half-cleared undergrowth, Nancy had emerged onto a patch of scrub at the foot of a limestone cliff, which reared a hundred feet above, bulging somewhat ear-like at the top.

A smudged and smiling Naw Bleh stood behind her.

To the left, and at the foot of the cliff in front of Nancy, fresh red earth spilt from the rock, mixed with vegetation washed by the recent rains. Emerging in several places, mostly towards the bottom of the landslide, just yards from Nancy - unmistakable - gold.

Saw Wah and Capt. Reh Doh entered the clearing, together with the soldiers.

"My Lord - oh my Lord!"

For a moment, they all stood staring.

The bodyguards were first to move up into the muddy tumble, heading for the most accessible chunks.

Holding her husband's hand, Nancy began picking through the mud towards a likely clump.

Saw Wah heaved on a glittering knob. There was a sucking sound, then - Plop! - in his hand a fist-sized ingot.

"Is that pure gold?"

"I don't know.

That's what it looks like. It's quite heavy."

"There's more over there!" - one of the village lads.

The two villagers scrambled elbow-deep in earth, semi-delirious. The Captain directed his men to likely-looking chunks.

"Gold! Weeee!" - Naw Bleh.

Nancy about to say something about the need to do this systematically. At least they should make a pile of ingots in the clearing, in case anything got lost. The captain had the same idea, at the same time.

Then something caught the corner of Nancy's eye. Slowly, mud sucking at her feet (in rubber boots), she edged up the mudslide. After a little finger-digging, she retrieved a small wooden box, decorated with mud-smudged gold filigree.

Nancy turned the box over in her hands, examining the fine workmanship. A familiar sickness in the pit of her stomach; pain shooting through her scars.

What is this?

She held the little box before her.

"What is this?" she asked no one in particular.

Capt. Reh Doh, a nugget in each hand, was about to give orders.

"Listen!" ... an intensifying whine, followed shortly by an explosion overhead.

Splintering cliffside - dangerously close.

"Mortars!" - yelled the captain.

Coming from the north –

"That way!"

There was smoke in the air, and at least one more explosion. The sound of gunfire, off in the distance - she's getting used to it now.

Nancy stuffed the box into her pocket.

Another explosion.

As she was blown backwards into Saw Wah's arms, Nancy caught a glimpse of wheeling black triangles, overheard. Knocking her husband off-balance, they tumbled - bouncing off small rocks, eventually squelching to a halt.

Clouds above, flat on her back, Nancy reached for Saw Wah's hand. She turned her head to see a small lump of dirty gold protruding from the mud, inches from his nose.

She squeezed his hand. "My darling, are you okay? Are you hurt?"

Saw Wah's hazelnut eyes flutter open. A broad smile.

"And you?"

Nancy let go of his hand, leveraging herself upright.

"I'm okay, I think."

Automatic gunfire nearby - judderingly loud. Nancy collapsed back on her bum, then sprang to her feet, beside her husband.

To their left, Capt. Reh Doh was pointing his M-16 towards the jungle. He let off two cracking rounds.

"What in the name of sweet Lord Jesus was that?"

Nancy and Saw Wah strained towards the treeline beyond. Something was moving through the undergrowth, between huge trunks and branches - something awful.

They were distracted by shrieks from above – a stream of bats pouring from fissures in the rock-face.

Nauseous again, Nancy staggered back as the cloud of bats wheeled overhead and cork-screwed screeching - a huge fanged creature at the head of the phalanx.

Down towards Nancy they came - a million twisting wings and tiny razor fangs. As the bats barrelled down, Nancy staggered backwards.

The creatures were all about her in the air –clawing, snatching at her - not biting ...

Nancy struggled to stay standing. Summoning all her energy –

"Be gone! Go away!" –

A wave of power pulsed through the creatures.

Momentary stillness - and then the bats recoiled, squealing back upwards in an inverse spiral.

"You so-and-sos!" - Nancy was never one to swear.

The bats were receding.

Nancy's first instinct was to retrieve the little box and open it. Sandalwood, with a tiny gold catch.

Twin plump rubies, on a bed of red silk. Nancy stared for a long time. Saw Wah had to dig her in the ribs with his elbow.

By now, the bats were gone. Nancy had a few nasty scratches, but otherwise was fine. She stuffed the rubies in her pocket.

It was almost dark. A few fat drops of rain.

Nancy calling down below - "Captain! What's going on?

Has the fighting stopped?"

Silence in the jungle. Creak of bamboo. Pit-patter of rain on huge leaves.

"I don't know Nancy. I wouldn't call it fighting.

Another surprise attack!

You'd better get down here.

Get behind that rock. Over there - both of you.

Come on, now.

If they come again, probably from that direction" - indicating the far side of the glade. "Stay behind me and the men."

Nancy checked the rubies in her pocket. She and Saw Wah began to pick their way down the mudslide.

"But where is Naw Bleh?"

A movement on the edge of vision. Something was moving again in the forest, just beyond the tree-line, past the three Karen soldiers.

Another crash echoed off the limestone rocks. Machine-gun fire, two or three hundred yards up to the right. They could see the muzzle flashes.

Capt. Reh Doh and his men in the middle of the clearing - their rifles pointed to the tree-line. Saw Wah frozen in mid-step.

Something massive black and evil was expanding into the clearing, looming out of the forest. This was the enemy - but not soldiers. They were still firing far off to the right - little orange flashes in the jungle.

An awful hush. A shimmering figure emerges from the treeline.

The Count!

A paralysing fear strikes them all.

A crack of thunder - moments after, lightning - then lashing rain.

The soldiers stagger back, figures distorted amid the rain - the whistle and crash of more mortars.

An explosion very near, thudding into the earth - mud and debris flying. Screaming from somewhere.

Nancy is still standing.

Saw Wah is shouting something, though he stands just inches from her –

"... dear - my darling - come on! Come on!

We have to get away."

Another huge explosion, very close. Nancy is thrown backwards, the air knocked out of her, crashing into mud and rocks. She regains consciousness almost instantly - blinks. A searing pain across her forehead.

Where is Saw Wah?

There is blood down her right side; she knows it's his.

Smoke everywhere. Where is he?

Nancy staggers to her feet, still looking around for her husband.

Then sudden horror. There he is - sprawled face down on the ground, yards ahead of her - covered in blood and dirt. A wisp of smoke in the air.

She must go to him.

A jab of pain through her legs, stumbling down the muddy bank towards her husband – and the looming terror.

A few yards to the edge of the clearing – through sheets of rain and crashing thunder. Nancy forced herself forward.

Oh where was Saw Wah?

There was the Count – growing impossibly taller and blacker by the moment.

Nancy felt the thrust of fear - staggered back a pace.

Then onwards again - between the Karen soldiers frozen wide-eyed. She willed herself onwards - towards the vampire. Pulsing blackly before her, the Count drew upwards.

She stepped forward once more. Terror in the rain.

Oh Lord protect us.

The creature was almost upon her – rearing hugely, a deathly pulsing shroud – ready to swop.

White fangs glistened horribly.

Everything is going in slow motion - backwards and forwards at the same time.

The Count suspended in mid-air, mid-strike - hate and the joy of hatred - black-winged death. Imminent annihilation.

Nancy gave herself completely to God.

"Jesus Christ, son of God, have mercy."

A stillness.

The vampire suspended in mid-air - above Nancy.

Unable to touch her – her Sacred Heart. Luminous clarity of Grace.

A shriek tears from the Count.

Silence again, and the echoing scream.

Crack of lightning.

The Count shimmers - recedes – collapses through black fractals back to the treeline.

At the edge of the forest, the Count looks back, snarling - fangs and pink spittle - hate-filled golden eyes.

Nancy is elated, confused, exhausted, grateful. She stands her ground.

At the treeline, the black-caped figure - now gone.

Rustle of the evening wind.

Nancy inspects herself - looks for her husband.

She seems to be okay. Where is Saw Wah?

She sits unsteadily on a newly dislodged boulder.

Is the Count really gone?

Nancy knows she has not vanquished him – but he could not take her. Something outrageously unique in the vampire's experience - he cannot destroy her, cannot touch her. Not tonight, anyway. This she intuits.

And now she is so tired, now the pain.

Nancy's forehead throbs hot black iron.

She must focus.

"Oh where is Saw Wah?"

She gazes uselessly, side to side across the little grove.

Another wave of pain. Nancy passes out.

...

She didn't see what happened next.

The captain clears his throat, reaches for a cheroot.

A thin and distant wailing. Delicate twang, almost on the edge of sound. Rain amid dimensions.

The sound is closer now, sweetly modulating through the clearing. A blanket of golden-green radiance, suspended in the gentle rain.

The soldiers and their captain are coming to themselves, as are the two villagers - cowering in the bushes. They stagger, try to focus.

Nancy is propped against a small rock, unconscious (although they don't know that).

There is Saw Wah - slumped at the edge of the clearing, not far from where the Count departed - spreadeagled in blood and dirt. He looks dead.

A crack of bamboo at the edge of the forest. A gentle radiance suffuses the clearing.

The rain has stopped - sun peeks through clouds. Water drops plop.

Ten-foot tall, silky white – the De Breh sways gracefully into the sun-dappled scene.

The De Breh is covered in long golden hairs. Graceful and obviously very strong. He lopes to the centre of the clearing, bends over Saw Wah.

A gentle humming in the breeze.

The De Breh pauses, then rolls Saw Wah onto his back. Leans his face close to the human's.

Silence in the dell.

A plosion of breath upon Saw Wah's face - sweet green De Breh spittle.

The De Breh straightens, surveys the little group of Karen. Somewhere in the distance, a peal of thunder.

Saw Wah stirs, sighs deeply.

The De Breh turns and ambles toward the edge of the clearing, slips back into the forest with a rustle - last glimpse of golden fur.

...

Nancy gasps – jolts upright, eyes open. First thing she sees is her husband.

Saw Wah breathes in, tries rolling onto his side, half sits up - drops again. He pauses, rolls to his other side, feels for damage.

Despite some tenderness, there doesn't seem to be much in the way of wounds. That's strange - because he is covered in his own blood, much mud, some twigs, and dollops of De Breh spittle.

Nancy staggers to her feet. Her throat is dry, but -

"Oh my darling!

Oh my dear Saw Wah - you are all right?"

He stands.

It seems he is.

That broad smile – Saw Wah strides towards Nancy, and takes her in his arms. This time she doesn't swoon, but wraps herself around her husband.

Not far off, Capt. Reh Doh rocks gently on his heels, head in his hands. The others stare dumbly.

A gentle rain starts falling.

Naw Bleh emerges from behind a nearby boulder.

"What happened?"

...

Late that night, they take stock

Nancy is badly scratched - but alive and safe, it seems.

Saw Wah's clothes are shredded.

"That's shrapnel does that" says Capt. Reh Doh. "That mortar came down right next to you - threw us all over the place, and we were yards back. Mud and rocks everywhere!

Private Eh Doh got a nasty cut. He'll be all right though.

I think."

Saw Wah is drinking tea from a blackened kettle, across the hearth from the captain - who stares at him, theatrically rubbing his eyes.

"For someone who seems to have lost so much blood, you are strangely - er - restored, young fellow.

No wounds at all, you say?"

Naw Sae Ler doesn't understand how, but his blood pressure is normal. He never felt better.

Nancy and Saw Wah wonder what this means. They thank God.

"My husband - saved by the Deh Breh!"

Saw Wah likes the sound of that.

"Well yes, I suppose so.

But what about that ... thing?

The Count.

Was that the Count?"

"Yes - that was him.

But what has become of him - I don't know.

It seems he couldn't kill me.

Blessed Jesus protect us all."

"Ahmen" said Saw Wah.

Nancy smiled softly.

"I must kill him. You know that.

If not sooner, then later.

Oh Lord."

She sipped more tea.

Nancy remembers the two plump rubies, feels for them in her trouser pocket. Soon she will have to find a better hiding place. Not that box.

But for now she is so weak.

...

For two days Nancy rests, not far from where VH is recovering. Saw Wah and Naw Bleh take turns by their bedsides, while the Captain supervises recovery of the gold.

The villages are busy. But for once, the captain has promised cash payment, and there is plenty of food and a little beer. And best of all - they've all heard about the De Breh.

On the third morning Naw Sae Ler pronounces VH strong enough to travel. Two hammocks are slung under bamboo poles. Four villagers will carry him back to Dwey Kee, and then to the road; two more locals lead the way and help with their kit.

Nancy walks most of the way, and is very tired by late afternoon. Saw Wah carries both their packs, singing quiet hymns along the way.

VH still cannot walk more than a dozen or so paces – but at least now he is lucid, and eating properly. There are large stretches of the last several days which he says he cannot remember.

Col. Philip will send his Landcruiser to collect them - the Captain's vehicle having been requisitioned to carry the gold.

One more night under the stars.

...

A couple of days later in Papun, Philip sends for Nancy and Saw Wah. They meet at brigade headquarters, in a timber and concrete block, partly built into the hillside. Several dozen automatic rifles stand oiled in racks along two sides of the room. Philip is in combat uniform, Colt-45 holstered at his side. On his green beret, the Karen National Liberation Army's drum and bugle emblem.

"Well, dear Cousin - you look a lot better than when you got here. You probably don't remember - you were pretty woozy - and so pale.

Now you look more hearty. Right, Saw Wah?"

"She does indeed, Colonel."

Nancy wasn't having this - "Dear cousin, I remember our arrival quite clearly, thank you.

And also of course your kindness to our little group.

I was feeling better then, and even more so now!"

They had spent the last two days as guests (in his absence) at Philip's nearby private residence. His kind and comely wife made Nancy and Saw Wah very much at home, and kept a healing eye on VH, who enjoyed sitting on the veranda in an old teak armchair.

Philip took a message on his phone, before returning his attention to Nancy and Saw Wah.

"Good, good.

You leave tomorrow first thing, correct?" One of those non-questions.

"Make sure you take that troublesome fellow with you. And by the way, he's not a regular journalist, you know. The ones who write full-time for a living – even longer feature articles - they usually don't stick around so long. Or ask those kind of questions.

I don't say that I don't like him, or even that I don't trust VH. But -

He writes all those articles and books, but he's got other agendas too. He's not a real 'professor', you know. It's what they call an honorary title.

We think he's MI-6, or the Dutch equivalent.

Anyway - I'm sure he's grateful to you. As am I."

Philip smiles, naturally.

"That is kind of you, and him.

Do recall though, it was VH who found the gold."

"Perhaps - but you know it wouldn't have remained hidden for long. Sooner or later, the villagers would have come across it. Or our lads – probably not the enemy.

Very good we've got it, anyway.

And you did retrieve VH.

So, well done."

More tea.

"The part of the story I do understand is - someone moved the gold out from that tumble-down mansion and up into the hills, at the end of World War Two - correct?"

"That's right."

"So the gold was moved, then uncovered last week by the landslide. Seems reasonable. I suppose.

As for the - er - other incidents, your husband has told me about ...

Well - none of it makes any sense. I would think he was raving, but he seems an otherwise sensible man. Also, Saw Reh Doh gave more or less the same account.

I couldn't get any sense out of your niece."

"Oh Philip - thank you so much for helping her."

The day before, Philip had sent a car and minder (a not-too-stern Karen auntie), to transport Naw Bleh back to her folks. She had left a lovely thank you note for Nancy, and they hoped to meet again one day.

In the meantime, Naw Bleh had been instructed to keep quiet about recent events.

Who knows what tales she was telling by now, back home in the village.

Philip took a spoonful of tea-leaf salad - "The official version is that you were ambushed by stragglers from that marauding column. They seem to have had one or more foreign mercenaries among them."

The KNU would take the gold. They reckoned at least $50 million. That would purchase a few ground-to-air missiles, and plenty of drones and explosives.

"Which we will need. Next week we attack Shwe Kyin.

Pray for us, dear Nancy.

After that, God willing, we will sweep down the Sittaung Valley - into the swamps and the sea. Let them rule the crocodiles.

Swear that you will keep it confidential, until you hear about it in the news."

And so they did.

...

Back in Chiang Mai, Nancy and VH recuperated for a few days more. Nancy's bat scratches were healing, and VH seemed in his right mind. He spent a lot of time sleeping, and writing.

VH passed on some tips to Nancy and Saw Wah. Certain elements of vampire lore and mythos. A silver medallion called Kilda Barry Ben. (Nancy knew that this was important, but she wouldn't find out why until the next adventure.)

They would meet again in London. They knew that this was not over – but agreed to stick with Col. Phillip's version of events, for now at least.

"Nancy – you know that the Count's agony is compounded, while Broglin keep lies half in ruins."

...

Before returning to London, Nancy and Saw Wah visited the HARD offices once more. They passed on a message from VH, who would lobby for an increase in Dutch aid to the Karen. Nancy and Saw Wah promised to be back in Thailand soon.

"That's good", said Kevin.

"You'll find that things have changed a bit in England. You know, food prices have doubled this past year - and since the last floods some parts of London are home only to rats."

...

After praying in the departure lounge, they walk hand-in-hand to the gate. Nancy felt the two large pigeon-blood rubies in her trouser pocket. Packed safely in checked luggage was an exquisite carved jade dragon, which Saw Wah had found amid the mud - to go with the white tiger.

Nancy seems to be the only person who can handle the rubies. Anyone else, it makes them sick. Two different Chinese merchants had said they didn't want the stones, although Nancy knew through Phillip's connections that each had the money. Oh well – she had not really meant to sell them.

One of the old gem traders had muttered something under his breath.

"Did he say the rubies were cursed?" Somehow Nancy knew he did, although she spoke no Mandarin.

Saw Wah winced at the recollection of nausea. Those horrible things.

Nancy knew it was her responsibility - her fate - to mind the two strange stones. At least until she knew what to do next. God would provide. She squeezed her husband's hand.

Saw Wah looked at Nancy, and knew that everything would be all right.

Only after take-off did he reflect that airport security had not detected the glowing rubies. Nancy had somehow known that it would be okay.

...

A hundred miles to the west – a shaft of moonlight on damp rock floor.

A filthy pit, in a stinking bat-shit cave high up a cliff-face, fifty miles south of Papun, not far from Three Pagodas Pass.

The Count, groaning, drags himself awake. He half-rises, retrieves a little wood and golden box - sinks back among the ashes and putrefying remains of last night's meal. Re-settles himself.

In each palm, six rubies glow weirdly in the semi-dark.

A ragged Familiar squats gibbering in the shadows.

A huge black bat wheels overhead.

Many thanks to the wonderful Naw Jacqueline, and to Mike and Siobhan. Thanks also to Ko Zaw Oo for the cover design, to Myo, and to Michi, Andreas, Charles, Dave, Deborah, Tom, Andy, Khun Chanida, and to Naw Benjawan and family. And thanks to Naw Bellay, and the three amigos.

Frogmort Press
Be human – real books, no bots

In solidarity with and to support the people of Burma, please consider donating to –

Free Burma Rangers

https://www.freeburmarangers.org/donations/

Bright Stars Maternity Bags Project

https://thr5ve.org/initiatives/bright-star-maternity-project

A portion of profits from this book will be donated to the FBR and Bright Stars.

For somewhat less fanciful analysis of ethnic politics in Burma, see –

www.AshleySouth.co.uk

Coming Soon!

Nancy and the Count: the cthnonic crypts

From lost cities in Burma, to the bowels of the British Museum – Book 2 of *Nancy and the Count* features your favourite characters, and more.

From stinking secret places around the world, the un-dead are stirring.

As Yangon and London flood, Nancy and Saw Wah must again battle the dastardly Count and his minions.

The legendary Naga is re-emerging from millennia of sleep, deep below the ground. Which way will the dragon turn?

Kilda Barry Ben.

FM
FROGMORT PRESS

FM
FROGMORT PRESS

Milton Keynes UK
Ingram Content Group UK Ltd.
UKHW052146021123
431840UK00002B/18